Spring Break

LC Kanon

Copyright

1

"I can't believe you read that garbage," Gia said in a loud voice, strategically crossing her arms to emphasize the lowness of her top. She paused, looking around to see if anyone noticed.

"I'm sorry, were you talking to me?" Eva replied, knowing the comment was directed at her but still pretending to read the *In Touch Weekly* she had in front of her.

"I just think it makes you look stupid," Gia countered, shaking her blonde curls casually with one hand.

An airy voice interrupted the tense banter.

"The only person who can make you look stupid is you."

This nonsensical comment came from Joy, drawing the blank stares of the entire clique.

The foursome was seated at a departure gate at Phoenix Sky Harbor International Airport, with only one girl declining to enter into the fray. Leigh sat motionless, looking at her own magazine with a frown and pretending not to hear the rumblings of a meltdown.

Gia, pack ringleader and mean girl extraordinaire, had gone on the offensive moments after the friends from Arizona Southern University took their seats. Wickedly beautiful, with blonde hair, blue eyes, and a model figure, she had dressed that morning ready for her beach vacation—meaning she had on barely any clothes to speak of.

Gia shifted in her short jean skirt, her bare skin making an obnoxious noise on the faux leather seat. Glancing to one side she smiled at Joy, who was positioned next to her. The two had been friends since Xavier prep school, long before either Leigh or Eva was on the scene.

Extremely beautiful and incredibly stupid, Joy was fiercely loyal to Gia, who she mirrored in looks and appearance. But while

Gia's hair was so blonde it was practically white, Joy had shiny, chestnut hair that could be in a Pantene ad. Today it hung straight as a pin, and Joy tossed it carelessly while rifling through her oversized bag.

Eva, the one with the offensive reading material, sat opposite this twosome. She was the only girl whose skin color was due to genetics and not a tanning bed. Growing up in South Phoenix, Eva had been one of many Mexican girls. But in this clique, she was the *only* one. Eva warily glanced at the two girls opposite who merely stared back, filling the air with tension.

Next to Eva sat a still silent Leigh. Adjusting her own dark brown—almost black—shoulder length mane, Leigh began flipping through her magazine. Never able to get her milky skin the deep, desirable tan of the group's signature look, Leigh had applied an extra layer of spray tan before leaving for the airport that morning. Anxious for any distraction, Leigh studied her legs, noticing a spot she had missed.

Leigh was a longstanding member of the group, having met Gia freshman year when Gia attempted to copy off Leigh during a written exam. Her clumsy attempt and Gia's disarming southern drawl were endearing at first. Leigh soon learned that Gia's father literally owned all of Tempe. This meant every Cardinal or Suns player knew who Gia was, and every club and restaurant welcomed her like a VIP.

Leigh reveled in her baptism into the A-list of the young, rich, and beautiful. And after a few months with Gia and Joy, it became clear that they shed "best friends" as quickly as they gained them. Somehow, through freshman year and beyond, Leigh had managed to stay on Gia's good side.

Through the years Leigh had seen the less fortunate girls bite the dust. Some of them were simply cut out of the group painlessly. Others underwent a kind of social torture which initially horrified Leigh. There were viral photographs and hate-filled social media campaigns. If there was a Nobel Prize for social torment, Gia would win. Leigh got used to it though, and had a history of sitting on the sidelines while Gia put her Machiavellian plans into action.

As so it went up until their junior year, when the neat little threesome of Gia, Joy, and Leigh was upended. After being introduced to Eva during a game of strip poker at their favorite frat house, Eva proceeded to lose the game—badly. And instead of ridiculing her, as Leigh was expecting, Gia latched on to their new acquaintance.

It seemed Gia couldn't get enough of Eva's exotic looks, so fundamentally different from her own. Unlike the other girls, Eva never went to private school, having grown up in a seedy area of south Phoenix. Gia didn't seem to mind, as Eva's value was in her looks alone. Eva was her new toy, and Gia was ready to show her off.

Show her off she did. That summer, Eva was a firm fixture in the group—present at every social, football game, and desert party. As the weeks slipped past, the four of them had jelled well enough to go into their senior year with one goal in mind: spend spring break in Cancun.

But something had gone horribly wrong. Gia had obviously taken a dislike to Eva, and it had nothing to do with what she was reading. Running through various scenarios, Leigh surmised it had to do with Gia's ex, Andrew, and his recent fascination with Eva. This was hardly Eva's fault, and they all knew that, but none of it mattered. She wondered why Gia had waited to strike until they left for their trip. Perhaps to prolong Eva's torment? In the tense moments that followed, Leigh felt a wave of relief she wasn't on the chopping block that morning.

Usually, they all hitched rides down to Rocky Point for spring break. But this year, Gia's father was flying them to Cancun as a special gift for his little girl. The destination? His timeshare at one of the city's hottest resorts, the Sol II. All the group had to do was cough up the cash for the food and drinks package, and then do what they did every spring break.

"I can't wait to lay out and drink," Gia sighed, flipping through her *Vogue* carelessly.

"I know. I really need to fix my tan," Eva muttered, testing the waters a bit. Too soon, Leigh thought, as Gia threw down her magazine in response. It skidded on the floor, landing with a thump at Eva's feet. The group sat, motionless, waiting for her next move.

"I'm going to the bar. Let's get a margarita," Gia sniffed at Joy, who rose in response, adjusted her tiny skirt, and swung her purse onto her shoulder. Gia shot a look at the other two. "Watch our stuff."

As Gia and Joy exited towards the bar, Leigh shot Eva a glance. Leigh didn't want this latest outburst to impact her standing in the group. She was less than enthusiastic to be leaving that morning, and now Gia's bad mood had further reinforced this opinion.

The guy Leigh had her eye on finally friended her on Facebook and was sending extremely flirtatious messages. It had been three months since her last boyfriend and the other girls were starting to notice. Now with leaving for a week, she would have to wait to pursue things until she got back. Leigh bent over to retrieve Gia's discarded *Vogue* and began flipping through the pages.

*

"I cannot stand to look at that little slut one more fucking time," Gia proclaimed, sucking down the margarita as properly as a Paradise Valley princess could. "I cannot believe she had the balls to show up this morning."

"I have no idea how she could afford it in the first place," replied Joy, rolling her brown eyes and tossing her long hair behind her for good measure.

"Oh, I'm sure she's real connected Joy," Gia said, adjusting her straw to break up the last bits of the frozen drink.

"Oh?" sniffed Joy, confused as to why Gia wasn't playing by the rules. The whole point of sneaking away was to talk about the other two.

"Yeah. To our cab driver," Gia replied, laughing. Joy giggled at the joke, before surveying a glassy-eyed Gia carefully.

"G, did you start without me?"

Gia opened her designer purse and shook the small vial of prescription medication.

"Joy baby, sometimes a drink just isn't enough."

Joy quickly rooted through her own purse for the pills she had found in her mother's medicine cabinet. After the bartender came over, she eagerly grabbed the second drink.

*

They barely made the plane. Leigh had to cajole Gia and Joy, now seriously inebriated, onto the jetway while Eva shuffled stoically beside them. The stewardess was the second obstacle. She refused to let Gia board—not due to her physical state, but because her skirt was entirely too short. It took every play in the book to keep Gia calm, though Leigh assumed another barbiturate was up to the job.

At last, Leigh convinced Gia to pull down the skirt a few inches and they were allowed to board. Joy followed them, giggling, while Leigh eased Gia into her first class seat.

"You're lucky you're rich," Leigh said, securing Gia's seat belt.

"You love it," slurred Gia, slumping back into her seat before closing her eyes. Leigh and Eva headed into coach, while Joy took her seat across the aisle from Gia.

*

Eva took her seat a few rows from Leigh. As she settled herself down for the short flight, she pondered her situation. What did she do to get Gia so upset? Eva felt her heart beating faster as her mind fell to the only obvious reason.

Andrew.

But it had been forever since Gia and Andrew dated! And besides, he pursued *her*. She hadn't been looking to hook up with Gia's ex. It just sort of . . . happened.

Feeling a knot rise in her throat, Eva considered Leigh's silence during Gia's earlier outburst. Leigh was the only one who might be sympathetic to her plight. But it was clear from Leigh's silence that Eva wouldn't be getting any help from that department.

No, she better think of something to get back into Gia's good graces. And end the liaison with Andrew—before Gia found out. Eva spent the rest of the flight in a fit of nerves, leaving the *In Touch* in her purse, unfinished.

*

Soon after taking her seat, Leigh found herself drifting off to sleep. She stayed asleep for the duration of the short flight, waking only when the plane began circling to land. Sitting up, she asked the woman beside her to put the shade down to hide the blinding sun. Fumbling for her things, Leigh hastily found her sunglasses as the plane landed, and prepared to disembark.

The humidity was pungent as the group exited the plane. As Gia and Joy came off their highs into very crabby and unpleasant lows, Leigh guided them through immigration as deftly as she could. She directed the group straight towards the most attractive immigration agent, who flirted his way through the interview. It wasn't until customs that Leigh felt a glow of anxiety, eyeing the stoplight-style checkpoint placed at the exit as they gathered their bags.

She watched passengers press the button to exit, and in response the light flashed red or green. Green means go. Red means stop. Heart pounding, Leigh took her place in the long line, watching the colors flash. She watched as it turned green for everyone in front of her. Suddenly, it was her turn, and she hit the button.

Green.

"That part always makes me so fucking nervous," she said to no one in particular once the group was all assembled. Eva looked up, appearing worried.

"You ok, Eva?" Leigh asked, pulling her hair into a low ponytail.

"Yeah, I, I mean, we're good," Eva mumbled. "I'm going to go find our ride," she continued as she walked away.

"What is with her?" grumbled Joy, flipping through her phone with a sour look on her face.

"She's looking for her dad, the bus driver," Gia sniped. Joy dissolved into laughter while Leigh, smiling, took out her own phone. "Eva won't be staying with us much longer anyway," Gia continued, in a tone that made both Joy and Leigh look up.

Before Leigh could respond, Eva returned with a short man in a white uniform. Bags were whisked away, and the Sol II resort bus slowly filled with holiday revelers.

"Fucking hot," Gia whispered behind Leigh, as they passed row after row of at-attention coeds. Her skirt was inches shorter by the time she plopped down in a seat near the back of the bus. As Eva approached the seat next to Gia, she was met with a decisive eye roll. Eva resigned herself to the row opposite as Joy took her rightful spot next to Gia with a smile. Leigh slid into the empty seat next to Eva.

"Tired, hungry," she said as she plopped down, offering what amounted to a feeble olive branch.

"We can eat when we get there," Eva whispered. Leigh glanced at Eva, who looked genuinely troubled. It was now very clear that Eva was next on Gia's shit list, but Leigh didn't have the heart to tell Eva what to expect. Besides, there was no way she could step in—Gia would have her head for it.

Resigning herself to an awkward silence, Leigh closed her eyes. She began nodding off again when the bus hit a pothole. Opening her eyes, Leigh saw the arches of their resort in front of them, framed in gold by the setting sun. Leigh was shaking off drowsiness when she heard Eva speak in a low whisper.

"Why is she doing this?"

Leigh pondered this remark, unsure over whether to respond. It was a major faux pas to actually call out Gia's bad behavior for fear of retribution. Should she ignore it? Play dumb? She let a few seconds go by, feeling Eva tense up beside her. As the bus rolled to a stop, Leigh felt groggy, almost paralyzed. But then she heard the giggling opposite them and felt a surge of confidence.

"Because she can," she said succinctly.

Eva didn't acknowledge the response. She began gathering her things, taking her time to disembark. Leigh waited until Eva was ready, watching her controlled movements with pity.

Stepping off the bus, Leigh looked around for Gia and Joy. Locating them near the resort entrance, Leigh noticed the two holding court with three very handsome young men from Michigan State.

"It's the penthouse of the resort, basically," Gia finished as Eva and Leigh walked over. Gia adjusted her lip gloss, admiring her reflection. As she flipped the compact shut, she shouted out the next command.

"See you at 11."

After one young man bent to pick up Gia's bag, she flew into attack mode.

"Not necessary, Eva's relatives are here to do that," Gia snickered, as Joy erupted in a chorus of laughter. The boys looked around, confused, before departing into the lobby of the Sol II. Eva, mute during the exchange, turned to follow them into the resort, her bags having been secured by several men in crisp white uniforms.

Leigh walked beside Eva with Gia and Joy bringing up the rear. As her flip flops slapped down on the tile, she ignored Gia's latest taunt and sized up the Sol II. It was like many hotels in Cancun. The sanitized white walls and drunken, debauched tourists greeted them as they strolled into the lobby. They had arrived.

2

"Oh my God, you look amazing!" Joy intoned with her best Paradise Valley drawl.

"I know," Gia replied, eyeing her reflection in the mirror and adjusting the straps of her dress.

"You look nice, Gia!" Leigh interjected. She had entered the shared bathroom of Gia and Joy, and was sipping a margarita from a batch they had whipped up earlier. Leigh wanted to make clear that their coveted threesome was still intact. To do this, she had to flatter Gia as best she could, and avoid pissing her off. She hoped this wouldn't take too long to accomplish.

"Leigh, I told you I was wearing pink, what the fuck." Gia picked up her mascara and threw it across the vanity, where it skidded to a halt in a pool of spilled blush.

Instead of responding, Leigh sucked down on the margarita and adjusted a flyaway.

"Both of us can wear the same color, Gia," Leigh finally said, putting the drink down to adjust her short, pink dress. "Besides, yours is more hot pink."

"I guess you're right," Gia responded, but not before giving Leigh a decidedly unfriendly look. Gia turned back to the mirror and snatched the mascara, hastily applying more with vicious strokes. She had straightened her hair, which was normally curled into perfect waves. Her thin hourglass frame was outfitted in a figure-hugging dress, making her look like a delicate, albeit very tan, china doll.

Joy mirrored Gia's appearance like an evil twin, right down to the style of her very short dress. This was by design, as Joy's prized features, legs as long as any Victoria's Secret model's, were always displayed to full advantage.

Joy's only downfall, Leigh thought evilly, were nachos. As silence fell among the frenemies, Joy glanced at Leigh in the bathroom mirror. Leigh had chosen a bright pink bandage dress that displayed her slim, athletic figure. Frowning, Joy sucked in her stomach.

Continuing their primping, Leigh pulled her long, dark hair in her hands and gave it a shake at the roots. Her cool grey eyes stood out from her well-applied liner, and her full lips were nicely glossed. While the rest of the girls were classically beautiful, Leigh's unique features and lithe figure made her the distinct outlier.

Despite feeling more confident, Leigh couldn't get Gia's cryptic statement about Eva not being here much longer out of her head. She had to know what Gia had up her sleeve.

"Hey, G," Leigh began, watching Gia in the reflection of the mirror.

"What?" Gia responded, narrowing her eyes to get a better vantage point with her mascara wand. Leigh paused for a second, and then continued.

"Why is Eva leaving soon?"

A slow grin formulated on Gia's face as she paused, glancing at Joy in the mirror. Joy began giggling.

"What are you two up to?" Leigh asked, laughing nervously. She was usually in on Gia's "missions," and it was slightly distressing that neither had let it slip, as drunk and high as they had been earlier.

"Eva's been fucking Andrew, I know it."

"My Andrew?" Leigh immediately responded, thinking of her new, potential beau.

"No, idiot. My ex Andrew, *my* Andrew!"

"Oh." Leigh felt stupidly relieved, letting the minor insult slide. "How do you know?"

"I put his webcam on and recorded them." Gia could barely

contain her amusement at this confession, and she and Joy shared a decidedly evil cackle.

Leigh stopped fiddling with her hair and turned away from the mirror to look directly at Gia before speaking again.

"You did not."

"I fucking did."

"And . . . what are you going to . . . Gia, you haven't dated him in over a year."

"She's supposed to be my friend, Leigh, don't you know what that means? I guess not. I guess I'm the only one who does."

Leigh didn't respond immediately, as it slowly dawned on her how furious Gia had become. The hot pink of Gia's dress offset the red flush that began at her chest and ended at her runway-ready face.

Gia was mad. Madder than that one night when she poured a glass of beer on some poor Gamma pledge. Madder than when Andrew dumped her and then promptly slept with the president of Delta Delta Delta. Thinking quickly, Leigh carefully sidestepped this growing anger and directed it where it rightly belonged.

"So, what are you going to do to her?" Leigh asked, nervously flicking the salt on the rim of her margarita glass.

"You'll see," Gia quipped, as she turned back towards her makeup application. Joy caught Leigh's eyes in the mirror and smiled.

"Just wait until you see this," Joy said wickedly.

*

Leigh had a few drinks before the boys came. In fact, all of them did. The bottles of Don Julio went down like water, which they supplemented with copious amounts of margarita mixes.

As the drinking increased, so did the snipes toward Eva. Eva looked confused but tried to laugh along, though often looking to Leigh in alarm. Leigh did her best to try and change the direction of the conversation but Joy was having none of it, egging on Gia at every chance.

Leigh was almost relieved when the boys from Michigan State showed up, cranked in their own right and sporting funnels for additional revelry. Leigh focused her attention on a tall blonde, the most seemingly innocuous one. She learned from painful experience this was often the best option in these situations.

The most attractive, obnoxious guy in the group was immediately drawn to Gia, which they all expected. Music and rounds of flip cup followed at breakneck speed, until they all realized that as part of the turn down service, the hotel had turned on the hot tub. When Gia realized this, she let out a high pitched yell and headed for the back patio.

"Let's all get naked!" she cried, drunkenly pawing at her dress, now nearly hiked over her hips. The rest of the guests followed, Leigh clinging gratefully to her newfound beau, the name of whom she hadn't bothered to remember. The patio of the second story condo overlooked the resort courtyard with a devastating view of the beach below. Gia's father hadn't scrimped. There was a full bar and gigantic flat screen facing the hot tub.

"Let's watch something!" Joy giggled. Eva, not quite in the tub, dangled a leg in and looked nervous.

"Let's watch porn!" cried Gia, thrusting her glass high. This was too much for the boys, who erupted in a yell that was loud enough to startle Leigh from her drunken stupor.

By this point of the night she was so wasted that everything seemed to be happening in a haze. In fact, she felt like she was watching a movie. There was Joy, who left the hot tub and hooked her phone up to the TV. There was Gia, celebrating the impending video by downing a Tecate from the funnel.

In the same confused moment, her beau began making concentrated attentions to her that could no longer be ignored. Her saving grace from his wandering hands came in the form of a very clear video of Eva and Andrew on the flat screen before them, having sex on his dorm room bed. For a moment, no one responded. It wasn't until Eva turned ashen, and Gia dissolved into laughter, that one of the boys looked at Eva.

"It that . . . you? That's YOU! Isn't it?" yelled Gia's male companion. The commotion that followed was too much for Leigh. Ignoring the yells, she exited the hot tub and made a beeline to the bathroom. With the floor spinning up at her, she slammed the door, shutting off the noise from outside.

As she locked the door, she whirled around to face the mirror. She looked wild-eyed. Her mascara had run down to her cheekbones, which were white as the pristine resort walls. She bent down over the toilet and rid herself of the evening's beverages. Intending to lie down for just a moment, she drifted off to sleep.

3

Leigh woke up a few hours later at the base of the toilet, vaguely remembering people banging at the door, asking if she was okay. She glanced at the clock on the wall—it was just before 3 am. The condo was eerily quiet, and it appeared the boys had gone. After wandering out onto the patio, Leigh soon learned that this was not the case, catching one of the party guests having sex with Gia at a frenetic pace.

Dazed, Leigh stumbled into the vacant room she was sharing with Eva, retrieving the dress she had worn earlier, adjusting it over her still-soaking bikini. After washing her face in the sink, she pulled her hair into a loose bun. Her stomach gave a groan. Food. Now. Grabbing her room key, she departed for the beach, thinking of a food stand she had spied when they first arrived.

There were still people on the beach, and as she fell in line at a nondescript food stand, she recognized someone sitting near the shore. The figure sat isolated, her arms crossed in front of her legs. Taking her burrito with her, Leigh walked slowly towards Eva.

"Burrito?"

Eva didn't answer; she sat in a tightly twisted lump, with one brown arm crossed in front of her, the other hidden in the folds of her boldly printed maxi dress. She looked very delicate sitting next to the ocean, her skin a glowing brown, eyes bright with worry.

Leigh felt much worse for wear as she studied her companion, whose only indication of the night's revelry was in her slightly frizzy hair. Getting no response, Leigh plopped down and promptly began munching on her burrito, talking nervously.

"You know it's amazing how much I can eat, and I still stay skinny. I wonder how long that will last." After a few seconds of silence, Eva responded, still staring into the waves.

"For you, probably a long while," Eva said, balancing something in her right hand. As if on cue, Eva held it up for Leigh to see. The metal of the gun shined with an eerie glow from the streetlamp behind them.

"Where did you get that?" Leigh felt her stomach give a flip, and the last vestiges of the booze seemed to melt away. Eva spoke in a whisper.

"Some guys on the beach, they gave it to me."

"What did you give them?" Leigh shot back, eyes glued to the weapon.

"Gia's handbag."

"Oh no. Oh Eva." Leigh shook her head as she spoke.

The designer bag was a very expensive, sentimental gift from Gia's father. But all this didn't seem to matter as Eva raised the gun to her temple. Her brown hand was shaking, the lines of the gun a harsh contrast to the soft curve of her face.

"I can't go back," Eva broke out in a sob. "She's probably posted that video to Facebook now. She probably has it streaming online." Her voice broke in to larger sobs, but her hand steadied.

Leigh shot to her feet.

"At least your family will know," Leigh blurted out, standing close to her crouched form. The words confused the both of them. Eva turned to look up at her, meeting Leigh's intense stare.

"What?"

Leigh let the question fall into silence, as Eva lowered the gun to her side.

"Your family, they'll know how you died. We'll never know how my sister died. She just disappeared." I must be still drunk, Leigh thought to herself, I never tell anyone about Rachel when I'm sober.

"How old was she?" Eva asked, slowly conceding to the pull of the story. Leigh kept a close eye on Eva's hand, which was still

18

clenching the gun slightly. Leigh continued talking, stalling for time.

"She was 15. She left for school one morning and I never saw her again." Leigh paused, staring down at Eva, and continued. "But at least your family will know. If you did, you know, kill yourself."

Out of nowhere, this struck both of them as very funny. As they laughed together, Eva slowly released the gun. Leigh resumed her spot next to her, feeling her body relax.

"How do you know she's dead?" Eva asked, now totally distracted.

"How did you know Gia was going to fuck you over? You just know. I'll never see her again. I just want to know how she died," Leigh said, suddenly exhausted by divulging such a personal story.

They both sat there for a time, watching the waves move away from them. The burrito and the gun, now forgotten, sat in discarded piles in the sand. Leigh continued.

"Gia told me earlier today you'd be leaving soon. I wondered what she meant."

"I don't get it. Why? I thought her and Andrew were ancient history. She could have just told me to back off and I would have," Eva said, bowing her head, speaking to the sand. Leigh shook her head.

"I have no idea; she's always been this way."

"And you've always been her friend?" Eva asked, still avoiding Leigh's gaze.

"Yes," Leigh responded.

"Why?"

"I don't know."

"What are you afraid of?" Eva snapped, looking directly at her now. Leigh pondered her question, but instead of answering, offered up another idea.

"They're still drunk you know. We can hide their phones so they can't upload the video." Leigh wished that this was, in fact, true. She would hate to let Eva down now. Not after she sat by and let it happen. For the first time, she felt a sense of protectiveness toward Eva.

"I'm serious, they are both hammered," she continued, "let's go do it now."

"What do we do about the purse?" Eva replied, her initial spark of hope replaced by worry.

"We'll just say some guys stole it. We came down here for a burrito," Leigh said, piecing it together easily. "We took her purse because it had the room key in it, and they grabbed it and went running." Eva made no response.

"You can leave first thing if you want," Leigh offered. Eva didn't respond but stood up, Leigh following her lead. They were halfway back to the hotel when Leigh stopped them.

"Wait, go back and get that." Leigh pointed at the discarded gun lying in the sand. Laughing and shaking her head, Eva went to retrieve it.

Walking quietly back into their condo, they heard nothing but silence from Gia and Joys' room. Moving cautiously, Leigh pointed to their phones, discarded carelessly on the living room table.

Slinking onto the now-vacant patio, Leigh hid the gun in the base of a decorative flower pot, ensuring a good covering of moss and greenery. Eva fumbled with the phones, locating the video file and erasing it off each one. The phones then joined the gun in the convenient hiding place. Smiling at each other in collusion, they tiptoed back into their room and collapsed into bed.

*

"I want the fucking cops, on the phone, NOW."

From the tone and depth of her voice, Gia should have by all accounts woken up the entirety of Cancun. While her powers of recuperation were infamous, even Leigh was surprised at the soberness of her reaction to the missing purse. Only a few hours had passed after Eva and Leigh's return when Gia promptly woke and turned the condo inside out looking for her prized possession. Leigh, still bleary eyed from the night before, told Gia the fabricated explanation as Eva hovered behind Leigh like a ghost.

"I want you to call them," Gia spat at Eva, trying to push Leigh out of the way to land her verbal assault. As Gia lunged at Eva, Leigh thanked the Lord she hadn't yet realized her phone was also missing.

"You're the idiot that had the brilliant fucking idea to take my purse, I know it. Get them on the phone. Nnnnnnnow . . ."

"Ok, ok, I'm calling," muttered Joy, who had located the hotel phone. Gia abruptly turned, stomping through the living room and slamming her door. As Joy recounted the particulars on the phone, the girls surveyed the damage from the night before in the morning light.

The room smelled. Plastic cups were strewn underfoot. Chips and unidentified fluids sat in a huddle on the kitchen island. Someone's underwear was wrapped around a lamp. The door to Gia's room opened as she stuck her bright head out, face still red with anger.

"And call the fucking maid while you're at it. I'm taking a shower."

As Gia retreated into the master suite, Leigh pulled Eva into their room, situated opposite.

"If you want to leave, I suggest going now," she said, grabbing a scarf for her hair and turning to exit. Eva shot to attention.

"I'm staying."

The words so surprised Leigh she stopped midway through the door, turning slowly.

"What?"

"I said I'm staying." Eva looked at her calmly, gathering every last bit of dignity she had. "What's the point of leaving anyway? They probably have another copy of the video on their computers. Why wait until they come back and post it? Might as well stay and see if I can talk them out of it. Or make amends."

"Trust me, all that's wasted on these two. Especially Gia, she won't forget."

"Still, I want to stay," Eva responded, refusing to be swayed.

"So be it," Leigh said, resolving herself to one painfully awkward week.

This time, it was Eva's stomach that kicked in. She grabbed her purse and turned to Leigh.

"I'm famished, let's get something to eat."

Leigh and Eva enjoyed a silent breakfast together. When they returned to the condo, they were met with a few cleaning ladies and the hotel manager. Gia was in the process of interrogating him when they arrived. As they entered, he rose from the couch, introducing himself as Alejandro Jiménez.

Though they had essentially slept in last night's clothes, youth and beauty were on their side. His eyes widened at Leigh's appearance, and they only grew wider when Eva entered the room.

Leigh sized up his exquisitely tailored and very expensive looking suit, with shoes so shiny they gleamed like mirrors. He was older than them, but he couldn't be more than 30. Leigh looked over to Gia.

Though furious, Gia positively glowed. Her long maxi dress touched just below her platform heels, and her hair was secured in long gentle waves. Her heart-shaped face was made up to perfection, with a waxen, doll-like appearance due to the climbing humidity. She rolled her eyes at the peripheral sight of Eva, and demanded they continue the conversation on the patio.

Thus situated, Gia caught sight of the flat screen, turned to Eva, and smiled. Eva looked down at her flip flops, frowning. Her point made, Gia slowly turned her attention back to Mr. Jiménez.

"So, let me bring you up to speed."

Gia launched into a pretty tirade about the Sol II's responsibility to its patrons, her father's generous contribution to the resort site construction, and the lack of overall security. Jiménez was lucky to get two words in, which went on the endless loop of "most sorry" and "please forgive."

He offered what little could suffice to Gia: a gift certificate valid at Sol II's resort shops, and dinner he would host in his private dining room—all expenses paid. Gia balked at the dinner.

"Just the gift certificate." It was clear by her expression that she meant to only party with her American compatriots. Joy wasn't as quick to opt out. She had been eyeing Jiménez's imposing figure and shiny shoes since his arrival.

"Well, dinner can't hurt, G," Joy simpered, her doe-shaped eyes landing on his expensive-looking watch. Gia paused before giving in with a generous sigh.

"Fine, but have this place cleaned up before we get back," Gia said. Mr. Jiménez rose and from an exquisite black bag pulled a chilled bottle of champagne.

"Everything you say will be done, my compliments." He was almost out the door when Leigh remembered.

"Señor Jiménez, what about the police? Don't we have to file a report?" She hurried over to him when he stopped, turned, and gave Leigh a melting smile.

"Señorita, in my resort, we are the police." He smoothly bowed and grabbed Leigh's hand, planting a gentle kiss.

"Now if you'll excuse me," he stated, closing the door behind him with finality. Leigh stood staring at the door, her hand tingling.

"I cannot wait!" squealed Joy, taking off for the shower as Gia was busying herself with the champagne bottle.

"You two stay here while Joy and I go shopping," Gia said, looking up at Leigh with a grimace. "I guess you can join us for dinner."

4

"You should totally get that."

"I know, right? I need!"

"Ugh, those two are fucking pissing me off." Gia redirected the conversation, stretching the black synthetic fabric tight across her bust line, admiring the effect in the mirror. Joy grunted as she struggled to bring the tight black skirt above her hips.

"That's it," Joy moaned. "I'm going on a liquid diet."

"I mean, first of all," Gia continued as if Joy hadn't spoken, "did you see Eva this morning when she woke up? Horrifying. And Leigh has gotten so fucking thin. She looks like a lollipop. I have no idea why we hang out with them."

"Well, Leigh is cool," Joy replied, tentatively glancing at Gia. She slowly eased the skirt up and adjusted her underwear. Gia wasn't buying it.

"She used to be. Now she's gone all bitchy on us. Plus, how long has she been single? I think she's a lesbian. I should have known, what with trolling for women on Facebook."

"How did you . . . " Joy began, confused.

"I hacked into her account," Gia responded.

Joy let out a nervous laugh. "Wow, really? What else was in there?"

"Just an email about you being fat."

"What?" Joy's face was now flushed, skirt forgotten.

"Yeah, she and Eva were making fun of a picture of you from last spring's social," Gia said.

"That dyke bitch," Joy snapped, now upset, and seriously smarting from not being able to fit into the tiny skirt.

"I told you. I say we do our own thing this spring break, leave those lesbos to themselves."

"Sluts," Joy responded, grabbing her purse and casting the skirt to one side.

Gia smiled and walked out of the dressing room. "Oh Joy," she muttered under her breath, "so very gullible."

As the two made their way to the next store, Gia made a point to admire all the clothing Joy picked out. When they walked into an accessories boutique, she introduced a new topic.

"Her family's all kinds of fucked up," Gia said.

"Eva's?" Joy asked, frowning over a price tag.

"I'm sure Eva's, but also Leigh's," Gia continued, ignoring the friendly greeting from the sales associate. "Her sister, like, took off. They never found her."

"You mean she ran away?" Joy gave the sales associate a glance.

"I don't know, I mean have you met Leigh's dad? He's really fucking weird. Who knows what happened." Gia slipped a small jeweled compact in her bag after deftly removing the price tag. Joy followed suit, slipping a lipstick into her purse.

"Yeah, he is weird. I wonder if, you know, he ever did anything to Leigh," Joy said.

"It would explain why she sleeps around so much, daddy issues and all," Gia replied, slipping another compact into her bag. Joy's eyes followed Gia's manicured hands as she expertly plucked it from the counter and into her bag. Spying a few pairs of sunglasses Gia had been admiring, Joy deftly followed suit.

After looking around at a few more items, Gia flounced out of the store without a backward glance. Joy scampered after her in her teetering platforms, trying to keep up.

Before returning to the condo, the twosome decided to stop at the resort bar for some lunch. Gia pounded three tacos and a full basket of chips, stopping intermittently to dot at her cherry lips.

"So what are you going to do with the video?" Joy inquired, moving her food around the plate.

"Upload it," Gia responded, digging into more salsa.

"Sure, I mean, as soon as I find my phone," Joy responded.

"Hmm, I can't find mine either," Gia replied, looking down at Joy's untouched food. "Aren't you eating? Don't tell me you're turning anorexic too." Gia helped herself to Joy's plate as Joy blinked in response.

"No, I'm just . . . wondering. Our phones are missing, your purse got stolen. You don't think that they . . . would have taken them."

"God how pathetic, I never knew they were so desperate," Gia announced to the entire bar, moving a chip around her plate to scoop up a wayward piece of chicken. After cleaning her plate, she wiped her hands on her napkin with a flourish.

"You know I'm fine with people having less money than me, I really could care less. I get that I'm spoiled. I know I grew up in Paradise Valley and got a Benz when I turned 16, but that doesn't mean that because of my father's generosity people can steal from me. How fucking pathetic."

She pushed the plate away and grabbed the purse she had borrowed from Joy, removing a jeweled compact and plopping it in front of her friend.

"That one's for you." Gia said, smiling. Joy giggled, accepting it with a grin.

Gia began hastily scribbling out their room number on the restaurant bill, and then paused, turning to Joy. "Jiménez owes me big. We'll have them kicked out of the hotel or something. I'll tell him they stole my purse. Then we can really enjoy our vacation."

"G, that is an epic idea!" Joy drawled. "I'll go back and get ready, meet you at dinner?"

"Yeah, let me handle Jiménez first, I'll go early. You meet the girls at dinner, they'll have no idea what's coming." Joy nodded at this. "Now," Gia continued, wiping her face clean and adjusting her top, "let's hit a few more stores before they steal the rest of our shit."

*

Leigh spent a long time in the shower, letting the heat massage and soothe the tension that had built up since spring break began. As the water pounded her chest and arms, she slowly acknowledged a feeling she'd had since the vacation began: after Eva departs the group, she would be next. And when her time comes, she thought to herself, she would not go quietly. After mulling this over for a few moments, Leigh snapped out of it. After all, she had a dinner to attend.

Leigh spent what was left of the day getting ready. She picked out her skimpiest black dress and spent a good hour and a half with her hair and makeup. She was just finishing the final touches when she heard a knock at the bathroom door. Opening it, she found Eva dressed to the nines as well—looking every bit the Aztec goddess.

"Ready for the last supper?" Eva snickered, easing into the loose alliance they had established the night before. She entered the bathroom and leaned on the counter, delving into the one topic she couldn't stop thinking of since that night.

"I keep running the video in my head a hundred times. What's she going to do with it? How will she use it?"

"She wants you to stress about it," Leigh responded, adjusting her bra and admiring the view in the mirror. "She's banking on it. She's totally . . . "

"Cruel," Eva finished for her.

"Yes, cruel," Leigh agreed, as there seemed to be nothing else to say. Each settled in their own thoughts for a while, as Leigh adjusted her bra straps and fixed imaginary flaws. Turning, she faced Eva.

"Are you ready? Joy told me we are meeting her there. I have no idea where Gia is."

"I don't really care where she is," Eva responded. "I'm going to hit the ATM first. Come on, let's get this over with."

*

When Leigh arrived at the hotel restaurant, her concerns about being Gia's next victim were confirmed. Joy glanced at her briefly before pulling out a jeweled compact from her purse and examining her face. Leigh took out her own lipstick and began applying it before feeling a stab of confidence. Why shouldn't she have a little fun?

"So," she began, placing the lipstick back in her purse, "did you buy that or did Gia steal it for you?"

"What?" Joy snapped, looking up with a grimace.

"You heard me. That's how it starts, you see, she gives you gifts. Takes you shopping, it's all fun and games. But then she starts asking you to steal things for her. More expensive stuff, way more than just a compact." Joy wasn't so easily scared off.

"Gia is fucking loaded Leigh, don't act so jealous."

"She's not loaded, her father is. Gia's father has lots of money. Gia does not."

"You are so jealous, it's disgusting. Know what else is disgusting? Your dyke-ish habits. Yeah, I know all about that. And pretty soon, so will everyone else," Joy said, closing the compact mirror with a satisfied smile.

Leigh stared at Joy and felt a burn of embarrassment in the pit of her stomach. Instead of letting rise, she let it fester a bit, turning into a potent brew of a very different emotion. Anger.

"And when she turns on you, which she will," Leigh began,

speaking slowly and concentrating on each word, "I want you to remember this warning. Because when you take Gia's side, you suffer the consequences."

"I don't think that will happen," Joy sniped.

"I hope not too. But then again, I guess it depends on who knows her better." This drew Joy's gaze to her, and when their eyes met, Leigh gave Joy a smirk and turned to enter the restaurant. Her timing was perfect. Eva, having hit the ATM beforehand, was nervously waiting in the foyer.

"We're the guests of Señor Jiménez tonight," Leigh said to the host after Joy joined the two. The hostess nodded knowingly and led them down a maze of hallways. Joy sulked behind them, stomping her stilettos for full effect.

The room they entered seemed to be part of a private residence rather than an extension of the hotel. It was an open-air dining area which expanded into to a tiled patio. The space was tastefully decorated with colorful plants, a hot tub, and expensive-looking Mayan artifacts. Gia had already arrived, and looked positively radiant in a short dress and glittering jewelry.

As they entered, Mr. Jiménez was fawning over Gia, seated next to him on a low chaise. When his eyes fell on Eva, he smiled. Adjusting her straps nervously, Leigh glanced at two men standing at the other end of the patio. Moving next to Gia, she gave them an inquiring glance.

"Who are they?" Leigh asked.

"Do I look like I fucking know?" Gia sniped back, sipping a cocktail. Leigh assumed Gia had hit the pharmacy beforehand, watching her glassy eyes shift focus back to the drink she held in her hand. Not responding to the verbal jibe, Leigh instead studied the men, who were now advancing on the group.

They were shorter versions of Jiménez, their suits and accessories a quaint replica of his own. From Jiménez's brief introduction, Leigh caught the name of one of the men, Danny. Sporting a small ponytail, he had a pockmarked, yet handsome, face.

Danny immediately began chatting up Joy and Gia, drawing them to the other end of the patio to view an elaborate stone bias. Jiménez all but dominated his conversation with Eva. Leigh did her best to stick by Eva's side, glancing over at Danny from time to time. Although she couldn't hear what was being said, he was making her two frenemies giggle uproariously.

Eventually, wait-staff emerged and supplied jeweled cocktails in very large glasses. Leigh picked up what she assumed would be the first in a long line of drinks and had the distinct feeling that *they* were the entrees. But when they were led in to an adjoining dining room, dinner was indeed served.

As they circled around a long table, Leigh was careful to sit right next to Eva, whom Jiménez had directed to one end. Leigh could hear the chatter from the group seated opposite. The men were so engrossed in her friends, they barely looked up. Leigh focused on the food before her, making meager attempts to listen in on Eva's conversation with Jiménez.

The meal was awkward. There were several exchanges made from Jiménez to his men in Spanish, which flew over the heads of all of the girls. When they did so, Leigh looked at Eva hopefully, who nodded in the negative. Her Spanish was horrid, and besides, they spoke too quickly.

As more cocktails were served, the conversation between Jiménez and Eva grew more intense. Leigh found herself growing drunker with each cocktail. After what seemed to her fourth or fifth drink, Leigh looked around in astonishment.

How long had they been there—three hours? Four? Night had fallen, and Leigh could feel the pull of the tide mark the passage of time.

When the meal was finally over, the group went out to the elegant patio for yet more cocktails. Soft music hummed from invisible speakers. The humidity made the sharp smell of the liquor even more noticeable. Leigh could hear the rhythmic crashing of the waves, which instead of being comforting made the situation seem more claustrophobic.

By this time, Leigh found herself in solitary company. Danny and his friend had sequestered Gia and Joy on one end of the patio. Both girls seemed delighted at this, and even if they weren't, they were too drunk to stave off their advances.

For his part, Mr. Jiménez had quarantined Eva on a low chaise camouflaged by some strategically-placed foliage. Seated a few feet away, Leigh noticed Jiménez was doing the most of the talking, his low voice carrying into the night. Eva was not motioning for assistance, and was even shooting him several shy smiles.

Feeling the numbing effects of the alcohol, Leigh wanted to melt away entirely. She let her attention wander to a lit pathway exiting the patio. She got up with the intention of doing a little investigating, and maybe finding the bathroom.

No one noticed as she walked down the winding pathway, which ran parallel to the beach. She was invisible to the group as she disappeared behind the dining area, the pathway ending a few yards away in front of a large, windowless building. It was the same in appearance as the white-washed resort, and Leigh thought nothing of trying the door, annoyed to find it locked.

Walking quickly back down the little path, she noticed a boat rising and falling with the waves, just off the shore. This boat looked very fast, with clean lines and no clutter onboard. Finding everyone on the patio where she left them, Leigh walked up to Danny.

"Hi, sorry to interrupt," she began, as Danny continued his intense conversation with Gia. Leigh stomped her stiletto on the ground in drunken annoyance.

"Hello! I have to pee people!" she cried out.

Without turning, Danny shoved an electronic key card at her so he could continue speaking with Gia, who never looked up to acknowledge her friend.

Leigh snatched it from him, tracing her steps back to building and gently placing the key card on the electronic pad. The door opened with a click, revealing several more doors. Leigh opened each one with the same key card, her brow furrowing at all the security.

There were no doors in the entire Sol II resort, Leigh mused, which means this must be Jiménez's private residence. Intensely buzzed and getting hungry again, Leigh immediately located a very ornate bathroom in one cavernous hallway.

Flipping on the light, she attended to the necessary business and did some primping. Her unease with Joy and Gia, coupled with the inattention of the other dining companions, didn't exactly put her in the best of moods. Grabbing her bag, she exited, quickly realizing after a few turns that she had no idea how to get back out.

The twisting hallways didn't assist her drunken navigation. Further complicating matters was the lack of overhead lights, and Leigh wasn't about to go searching for a switch. She could only hear her heels clicking on the tiled floors as her eyes adjusted to the darkness.

"Oh this is it. This is the way," Leigh declared to the empty hallway, feeling her buzz give way to sobriety as she realized she was getting lost. Burying her growing panic, Leigh walked down a hallway she thought was the exit, only to find all the doors lining it locked. She advanced towards the last door at the end of the hall. Holding her breath, she placed the key card next to the pad. It chirped back at her with a green light and a click. With a yelp of success, she pushed the door open.

Weird, Leigh thought, as the room's cool air made her hair stand on end. Leigh kept walking forward, the lights coming on with each step. After a few tentative steps, all of the lights flew on, highlighting a very long, narrow room.

Surveying her surroundings, it took a few moments for Leigh to register what she was seeing. The room was packed to the ceiling with racks of small, white packages tightly wrapped in plastic. She leaned down to investigate and shot up just as quickly.

"Fuck me," she whispered. She knew what she had stumbled upon and immediately felt her stomach drop. Midway down the aisle, Leigh glanced toward the exit closest to her, a door located at the opposite end of the room. She made a beeline for it. Fumbling at the handle, she hastily inserted the key card, hearing the chirp of recognition as she pushed it open. Soon after entering she stumbled over what felt like a pile of rugs.

Leigh let out a tiny yell as she fell, landing in something wet and sticky. Pulling herself to her knees in the pitch black, she fumbled for her purse, located her phone, and activated her flashlight app. She followed the artificial beam of light to a shoe, then a leg, and then to a torso. Where she expected to see a head there was nothing.

A musty, metallic scent hit her like a brick wall, and she pulled herself slowly to her feet, shining the light on the rest of the room. There were eight or nine torsos, all without heads, all piled neatly on top of one another. Leigh felt the rush of blood in her ears, bile rise in her stomach. After a few moments, it subsided, melting away into a disturbing calm.

5

Leigh managed to stumble out of the room, past the rows of endless white packets, and located the bathroom. When she looked in the mirror, her pupils had dilated, and the pallor that had startled her earlier was replaced by a faint glow.

As she scrubbed the blood off her hands, she watched the pink trail flow down the drain. After exiting the bathroom the second time, she realized she must have been drunk. The way out was obvious.

Walking back to the dinner party, Leigh returned to empty plates and margarita glasses. Turning, she grabbed a bottle of tequila from the nearest patio table and retreated behind some oversized ferns, intending to have a seat on the beach and drink away the last 30 minutes of her memory.

She was about an inch into the bottle when she realized it was no longer just her and the waves. Someone had re-entered the patio area. It sounded like Danny, and it seemed he was having a rather unpleasant conversation.

Leigh, hidden behind the foliage, could feel his nervousness in the tense and halting sentences as he spoke into what she assumed was a cell phone. His conversation went on for a good 15 minutes, mostly dominated by the person on the other end.

The conversation abruptly ended and Leigh heard thudding footsteps moving away from her. It was then she realized she still had the key card. Tucking it in her purse, she slowly began tiptoeing towards the beach, bottle in hand. She followed the coast line all the way back to their room.

As she approached their condo from the beach below, she could see that the lights were on. From her vantage point, she watched shadows crossing in front of the patio door. A small voice told Leigh she should peak into the room from the patio, making sure it was safe before entering.

Emboldened by alcohol, Leigh tucked the bottle of liquor in the front of her dress, wincing as the heavy glass dug into her flesh. She slung her purse diagonally across her shoulders, and began climbing the decorative design on the outside of the condo.

As the resident queen of the Arizona Southern University rock wall, this was fairly easy. It only took her a few minutes of climbing before she deftly pulled herself up and onto the patio. Waiting a few moments to catch her breath, she could hear muffled sounds from within the condo. Slowly, she crept towards the patio door, removing the tequila bottle as she did so and holding it firmly at her side.

Looking through the glass door, between the vinyl blinds, she saw Gia and Joy. They were sitting on the couch, trembling, dark trails of mascara marking their cheeks. The man who was with them at dinner, the one whose name Leigh never caught, was shouting on the phone. Eva was nowhere to be seen.

Leigh leaned in closer to see if there was anyone else in the room. She noticed the door to her bedroom at the end of the hall was closed. A thud from behind the glass door made her jump. In the span of a few seconds, the man on the phone flung the glass door open, and stepped out on the patio, still yelling at his phone.

Leigh had just enough time to retreat into a dark corner, her back flush against the railing, heels hastily discarded. The man had his back to Leigh as he faced out towards the ocean. He was talking fast now, as if explaining something away.

She took a deep breath, and raised the tequila bottle with both hands. Swiftly, she closed the two steps behind him, and brought the bottle down on his head.

There was no satisfying smash, the bottle was made of such heavy glass that the reverberating blow nearly knocked Leigh off her feet. She reeled back with the bottle still in hand. The man sunk to the ground, one hand pawing frantically at the top of his skull.

The dent had taken a good bit of flesh and bone out of his head, a gruesome valley of red and white exposed within the polished blackness of his hair. Leigh took another breath, ignoring the pounding of the blood now rushing through her ears, and walked over to his quivering form.

She aimed right at that red crease, cracking it wide open as she brought the bottle down again, this time with a satisfying crunch.

The man stopped moving, his body crumpled forward, fingers now relaxed around the cell phone. Leigh placed the bottle down, her body humming.

She picked up the cell phone and held it to her ear, waiting breathlessly. After a few seconds of silence, a clear and direct question echoed from the phone in slightly accented English.

"Hello?"

Leigh held the phone away from her, staring at the receiver. Quickly, she shut it off and put it on the patio; raising the tequila bottle once again, she smashed the phone with the bottle. Sensing an audience, she turned. Gia and Joy were standing on the patio, staring at her with fixed, horrified expressions. Leigh spoke for the first time in the span of several hours.

"Where is Eva?"

They stared at her for what seemed like a full minute. Finally, Gia, rather than answering, glanced through the patio doors to the bedroom at the end of the hall. Leigh walked over to the flower pot and retrieved the gun she had hidden the night before.

If there was a response from Joy or Gia, it was muted. Leigh's head buzzed but her actions were quick and direct, almost as if she were on autopilot. Leigh let the gun fall comfortably to her side. In her other hand she held the bloodied bottle of tequila.

"Hold this, G," she said, shoving the bottle in Gia's hand as she walked past her and Joy. The living room welcomed her with an eerie silence. Everything had changed.

She removed the clip from the bottom of the gun, like her

father taught her to. The bullets, in perfect order, shined back at her. Closing the clip, she switched off the safety and checked the chamber. Finding everything in order, she took a firm grip on her weapon.

Joy and Gia had now joined her in the living room, with one of them at least showing signs of intelligent life.

"We have to get out here, now. Let's take a cab to the airport and . . . "

"What happened, tell me first," Leigh quickly interrupted Joy, turning to look at them with the gun gently resting on the kitchen island.

"Well," Joy began, eyes focusing on the weapon. She took a breath, swallowed and regained some confidence. "We were drinking after dinner when Jiménez got cranky, wondering what was taking you so long. Danny went to go check the bathroom and said you weren't there. That's when all hell broke loose. Eva said she wanted to go look for you, and Jiménez said he had other plans for her . . ." she paused. Leigh's heart was pounding, adrenaline coursing through every inch of her body. Joy continued.

"Danny went to go look for you and the rest of us came back here. Jiménez took Eva into her room. Then . . . the other guy took a phone call and started getting really nervous. After he got off, his phone kept ringing, he wouldn't answer. It was just ringing and ringing. It was driving us all nuts."

Gia, tears in her eyes, nodded her head in the affirmative. Joy continued. "He finally answered and started yelling. Then . . . you . . . Leigh, what did you do?"

A noise at the end of the hall saved Leigh from answering. Leigh hid the gun behind her back, and waited for the door to open. As if on cue it did, and a shaking, red-faced Eva appeared in the open doorway.

After closing the door behind her, she walked down the hallway to the kitchen. Slowly, she steadied her quivering form on the kitchen island.

"Gia," she began, "he wants Gia next." Eva leaned against the island, the words coming out in short bursts. Gia bolted for the exit, and Leigh, without thinking, grabbed a handful of Gia's thick hair. Pulling a squirming Gia to the ground, Leigh quietly spoke.

"Go."

"Are you fucking crazy," Gia hissed, twisting away from Leigh's grasp and yanking on her hair to free it. "Send Joy in to see him. Send Joy!"

Leigh released Gia, turning to Joy who blankly stared back. Joy began moving backwards. Leigh raised the gun, pointing it at her. Joy looked at Leigh, horrified.

"While not ideal," Leigh began calmly, the ringing in her ears getting louder, "there may be one way to get out of this. So Joy, I want you to go in there and distract him." She paused for emphasis. "Use your imagination. I'm giving you 20 minutes, and then I'm going to burst in there and blow his brains out."

"You're nuts, you're fucking nuts," Joy finally croaked out. "What the hell is wrong with you? We're all dead Leigh, these guys are going . . . "

A drunken shout came from the closed door of the bedroom. Eva jumped. Leigh took advantage of the distraction to advance on Joy.

"In the room. Now," Leigh demanded. Joy looked at her with horror. Eva let herself exhale and Gia, splayed on the floor, kept her eyes focused downward.

Leigh figured she'd have to threaten again, but slowly Joy walked away from the group, turning towards the bedroom. She hesitated at the last moment, but entered the room confidently, closing the door behind her. Leigh exhaled slowly and lowered the gun cautiously to her side. She looked at Eva, who was now visibly shaking.

"Gia, take Eva into the bathroom and help her out." Gia looked up to Eva's outstretched hand. "Oh never mind," Leigh replied, taking Eva's hand herself and leading her into the bathroom.

Guiding Eva to the sink, Leigh turned on the faucet, putting Eva's hands beneath it. Leaving her to watch the sink fill with water, Leigh returned to the living room. Gia was still in a crouched position on the floor. Leigh took her by the arm, pulling her up and into the bathroom before closing the door.

"Sit," Leigh barked at Gia, who sat down on the edge of the ornate whirlpool tub. Leigh turned off the faucet, grabbed a towel and dampened it, then gently wiped off Eva's tear-streaked face.

"Are you ok?" she asked. Eva nodded, brow furrowing.

"Are you?" Eva asked. Leigh looked back at her, grey eyes calm.

"How long has it been?"

"Maybe 10 minutes," Eva responded. She took the towel from Leigh and began wiping down her arms. "What are you going to do? You aren't seriously going to go in there and shoot him, are you?"

"Are you kidding? Of course not," Leigh responded.

"Then what are you going to . . ."

"I'll figure it out. Stay here. If I'm gone more than 10 minutes, call the embassy. Not the cops, the embassy." Eva nodded back.

Leigh exited the bathroom, pulling the door closed behind her. Quickly, she walked down the hallway to the bedroom Joy entered, putting her ear to it. Hearing nothing, she opened the door.

6

Joy and Jiménez were laying on the bed, deep in conversation. Leigh didn't hide the gun, which Jiménez did not appear surprised to see. In the precious moments she had, Leigh took in her surroundings.

The bedroom felt musty, claustrophobic—the weak light from a table lamp casting ominous shadows on the bed. A strong stench of tequila permeated the room, which was strewn with Jiménez's discarded garments. While he was lying angled towards her, Leigh could not see any weapon. That meant he must have it with him, at the ready. His first question threw her completely.

"So, who are you with? La Familia?"

"I'm not from any cartel," Leigh responded, after taking a few seconds to grasp what he meant. Señor Jiménez did not look so handsome now. The veins in his forehead pulsed, and his brown skin almost gleamed red. It was clear by his expression he did not believe her.

"So," he began, speaking at her in a mocking tone, "you just came on vacation with your girlfriends and start murdering the lieutenants of a very dangerous cartel?"

By his delivery and the bulging veins in his neck, Leigh figured he must be extremely drunk. This could be an opportunity or a risk. It depended on the man. Jiménez leaned forward menacingly, eyes bloodshot, growing angrier when she didn't respond. Leigh's mind flashed back to the bodies she had found earlier that evening. Surely, he didn't think? Did he think she was sent here to kill him?

She watched his weight shift slightly. His right hand was cradling the back of Joy's head, who was staring dully at Leigh with the tiniest smirk. His left hand was hidden by the folds of the bedding.

Leigh thought about the bodies, the white packets, and the valley of red in the man's head she had just murdered. She heard herself answer.

"Yes."

He threw his head to the ceiling and laughed.

"Wait until Guero hears this."

"Who?" Leigh heard the name and felt her stomach drop from both from fear and excitement. Her response seemed to make Jiménez explode. He leaned forward, eyes bulging, left hand still hidden. Leigh felt her body tense, felt the fingers around the gun clench with the thud of her heart beat.

"You already know, you fucking bitch. He will make you suffer until you beg him to kill you."

"Is he here now?" Leigh asked. Jiménez snorted and she relaxed just slightly. The answer was no, then. If this person he called Guero was here, Jiménez would be sure to gloat about it.

"You found out, didn't you?" Jiménez spat at her. Leigh's mind danced around a million different theories. The drinking, the overreaction to her missing. Maybe someone was feeling guilty?

What had Jiménez done, and where did this Guero enter in to it? Guero must be the boss, the boss of whatever cartel Jiménez was associated with. Joy moved slightly on the bed, and Jiménez looked down at her and smiled.

"We were making a deal, before you joined us. She was willing to sell you out, you know, for her freedom." Joy looked at Leigh with smug satisfaction.

"I knew she would," Leigh admitted. The words had no impact on Joy, but seemed to amuse Jiménez.

"So what do you propose?" he asked, massaging the spot on Joy's temple where Leigh had directed her gun only minutes before. He didn't wait for her response.

"I keep your friend," he chuckled, and Leigh knew he wasn't referring to Joy. She remembered Eva's pink face, her shaking body. He continued.

"Your friends enjoy their vacation, and then go home. They forget all about this place."

Leigh noted she wasn't included in the aforementioned deal. Apparently he was still under the impression she had been sent by a rival cartel.

"Say I leave," Leigh offered in response, "right now. I take my friends with me, we say nothing about any of this."

"Too late for that," he slurred back. "But you are crazy if you think I'm going to let you walk out of here alive."

"Say I just kill you and leave," Leigh snapped back, fingering the trigger of her gun. His dark eyes held a menacing glint.

"Threaten me," he began, his hand now visible at the edges of the comforter, and with it the glint of the hidden weapon, "and I kill your friend." He brought the gun to Joy's head.

Her grin was now gone, her body went limp, brown eyes quivering with fear. Leigh never took her eyes off Joy. After a few seconds of silence, Jiménez looked incredulous.

"I said I will fucking kill your friend."

"I heard you," responded Leigh, who raised the gun and shot Joy right between the eyes. Jiménez scrambled out of bed, screaming—blood from the bullet wound momentarily blinding him. His stumbling gave Leigh enough time to aim and fire several shots into his head and torso.

The gun was exquisite, smooth and precise, and the gunshots sounded more like the folding of a crisp sheet than bullets mauling bone and flesh. Jiménez let out a gurgle before dropping forward on top of Joy. Neither of them moved.

After taking several deep breaths, Leigh walked over to Jiménez and pried the gun from his hands. Placing it gently on the carpet, Leigh hastily located his cell phone, checking the pockets of his discarded clothing for anything else. There was a keychain that bore the logo of the hotel group, but no wallet. She found another electronic key card, which she tucked into her dress. Leigh stood up, never once looking at Joy, whose stillness suggested the bullet had ended her life instantly.

Exiting the room, she found Eva and Gia sitting in the living room. Gia was seated, staring at a blaring television. Eva had been glancing out at the patio, muscles tensed, when Leigh appeared. When Eva saw her, she jumped to her feet.

"Jesus, Leigh. We heard . . . we heard gunshots!"

Gia turned her head.

"Where's Joy?"

"He shot her," Leigh responded, not meeting her vacant gaze. Gia accepted this with a blink, and turned her eyes back to the television to resume her catatonic state. Eva stared at Leigh, and slowly nodded her head.

"And I shot him," Leigh finished, as Eva closed her eyes, holding her hands in front of her face.

"What are we going to do?" Eva asked, almost in a whisper. Leigh stood still as a statue, looking around in a daze.

"We have to leave."

"What about the bodies? Should we call the police?" Eva asked.

"We need to move them," Leigh responded, ignoring her second question. "Let's clean the room up as best we can. It's spring break, after all."

"This isn't funny, Leigh. Joy is dead," Eva responded, her voice cracking.

"These people have serious connections Eva," Leigh hissed, placing the gun and Jiménez's cell phone on the coffee table. "Remember what Jiménez said, they are the police!"

"Leigh, we can't just . . . "

"Eva, we have to leave."

"Ok, ok. Let me think." Eva slapped her hands together, discarding any rational course of action. "We call room service," she began, "tell them that Jiménez is here, and he wants the full spread. Tell them to leave their largest cart outside. Then we can move the bodies. But where . . ."

"I know where," Leigh responded, motioning at the phone for Eva to call and removing the key card from her dress.

After deftly executing their order, Eva hung up the phone. Rising, Leigh motioned towards the bedroom. They were halfway down the hall when a shrill ringing interrupted their progress.

"Is that your cell phone?" Gia called out from the living room, still in her childlike daze. Quickly walking back into the room, Leigh glanced at Jiménez's phone, which was buzzing with an obnoxious ringtone.

"No," Leigh responded. As Eva rejoined her in the living room, Leigh watched it ring once again before picking it up and hitting the answer button. She held it gently to her ear, giving Eva the universally acknowledged signal for silence.

"Hello?" she asked, more flirtatiously than she had intended. A few seconds ticked by.

"Who is this?"

"Just a girl, on vacation in Cancun," Leigh responded. The closer she could keep it to the truth, the easier it could be remembered. Didn't she read that in a detective novel somewhere? Several moments passed before the voice responded.

"Is this some kind of joke?" the voice said. The speaker was smooth, confident. Not the empty suave of Jiménez, but a threateningly self-assured individual. Against all her instincts, Leigh felt a slow burn in her stomach, followed by a flutter in her chest. What was wrong with her? She took a deep breath and closed her eyes.

"What does your instinct tell you?" she said, louder this time. There were a few more meaningful pauses on the other end of the line.

"If you really are on vacation, I suggest you go home. Go home right now."

"Not an option at this point," Leigh responded, glancing down the hall, dreading the task at hand. This time the answer was immediate.

"Why?"

"Because I just killed two of your men," Leigh responded, watching Gia curl up on the couch and cover her ears. Eva, by contrast, nearly jumped out her skin, mouthing obscenities at Leigh as she paced around the living room.

"You are lying to me," the man responded. Leigh didn't fill in the silence, letting him struggle on the other end. Moments slipped by. Feeling a pain in her chest, Leigh realized she had been holding her breath. Slowly, she exhaled.

"Well then," he finally responded, seemingly coming to a conclusion.

"Yes," Leigh responded, almost impatiently.

"If you've killed my men, I'm afraid I can't let you leave. In fact, I'm going to have to speak to you in person." Leigh felt her stomach twist into a knot.

"Oh, you'll let us leave all right," Leigh said. Eva was now thoroughly confused, staring at her friend with a proper mix of suspicion and anticipation.

"Why is that?"

Leigh could sense that he was getting a bit tired of the game, and his accent was getting worse and worse. He was getting angry.

"Because I've got a scoop for you," Leigh began, the words flowing easily. "The owner of the Sol II resort, the one who also works for a drug cartel, just raped two American girls. I have witnesses. Oh, and there's one more thing." She didn't wait for him to reply. "I want a lot of fucking money wired into an account that can't be traced, or I'm going straight to the media."

Eva's jaw dropped, Leigh couldn't help but smile. She must be losing it.

"We need to talk this over in person," the voice replied. Leigh felt the ball fall into her court. He was being too pushy—the game must be played slower.

"No, not yet. I think I need to show you how serious I am first." With that, Leigh ended the call. As she did, a knock on the door made them all jump.

"Just leave it outside!" Eva cried, flying to the door. Leigh crouched on one side of the door frame with Jiménez's gun, just in case, before Eva confirmed it was indeed their room service. Opening the door, they brought in the cart laden with delicacies. Eva looked at the food, and then at Leigh.

"What do we do now?" Eva asked Leigh, suddenly exhausted. Leigh shrugged.

"We eat."

7

They didn't expect to taste the food, but Leigh was surprised to find that she was starving. Gia was eating like she'd never see food again, wolfing down tacos and an entire plate of enchiladas. After she finished she started shaking, went over to the kitchen sink, and threw up. Eva took advantage of the distraction to get some answers.

"Mind telling me what that phone conversation was all about? All that stuff about wiring money into an account? What do you think this is, a movie? We are in some serious shit Leigh, and now you've just fucked with whomever that was on the phone . . . someone we know nothing about," she said. "He is probably dispatching the rest of his crew here to kill us."

Leigh chewed on her taco, deep in thought. Swallowing, she turned to face Eva.

"I didn't tell you what I found when I went on my little investigation after dinner. Let me enlighten you. Jiménez's own illicit store room, stacked with little white packages. And not only was he hiding drugs, I also found a room filled with headless torsos. There are no men to send, Eva, because someone killed them all."

"Who? You?" Eva asked, eyebrows raised.

"No, not me," Leigh replied, almost hurt. "I have no idea. We have to get out of here." She stood, anxiety getting the better of her. "I need some time to think."

"But no police? Not even the embassy?" Eva replied, slightly hopeful there was a quick end to their predicament.

Leigh's heart began pounding again. She should want to do the responsible thing, go right to the cops, the embassy. But she couldn't. She thought about the dead bodies in the bedroom. The bullet that killed Joy, which only could have been fired from one location, by one person.

"No, it's too risky." She looked up at Eva, feeling guilty. If Eva had reservations, she kept them to herself. Slowly putting her napkin down, Eva studied her cuticles for a time before looking up.

"Where are we putting them?" she said, resigned to their chosen course of action.

"With the others," Leigh responded, tossing her a key card. Eva caught it, eyeing the plastic card in her hand. Looking up, she motioned to the bedroom.

"Let's get this over with."

*

Transporting the bodies on the room service cart presented a challenge. They decided against piling them up in one load. Instead, they started with the man Leigh killed on the patio, placing him on the bottom rack in the fetal position, the white tablecloth neatly disguising what was underneath. Easing him out of their room, they wheeled him from their condo to the compound where their night had begun.

Leigh and Eva made another trip for Jiménez, who was so tall, his limbs and arms kept falling out of the cart. They hid their grisly task as best they could, giggling and laughing like drunks whenever a hapless employee stumbled upon them. Not one stopped them, in fact, most of them smiled good naturedly. Leigh chalked it up to the lateness of the hour, their seemingly inebriated state, and their scantily clad appearances.

It wasn't until they were ready to move Joy's body that Gia really started to lose it. Leigh had to shake her a few times before she helped, lifting Joy's limp body onto the cart, and covering the corpse hastily with several bathmats before putting the white room service tablecloth in place.

"Take whatever you need, we probably won't come back," Leigh directed, steadying the cart with one hand. After a cursory search of the condo, they stripped the beds, tucking the blood-stained linens under the cart for disposal. Before departing, Eva ran to the porch to retrieve the two cell phones they had hidden. She stashed these in her purse, rejoining Leigh for their final trip.

"If anyone called the police, they'd be here by now," Leigh said to herself as Eva nodded. "Let's put the 'Do Not Disturb' sign up, it will buy us time until they come and clean the rooms."

Eva followed her directions rapidly, slapping the plastic indicator on the door handle before taking her place behind the cart.

They followed the now familiar trail. Moving slowly, they made their way down a service walkway past the hotel restaurant, where it connected to the private patio of Jiménez's dining area. Winding down the path to the secret compound, Leigh opened the doors with the key card and eased the cart inside, with Gia following slowly behind.

Moving the cart down the narrow hallway, the two finally brought it to a halt before the room which held the final resting place of Jiménez and his unfortunate associates. This was the first time they had taken Gia along with them, who was showing signs of cracking. When Leigh opened the door with the key card, Gia found her voice.

"These people are dead!"

Ignoring her, Leigh and Eva systematically removed Joy's body from the cart, placing it on top of the pile of bodies with a grunt. After completing this task, both leaned against the wall, exhausted. Gia stared at them and continued.

"Why are you guys acting like this, we have to call the police. We have to . . . we have to leave. Now! What is wrong with you? I'm calling my dad."

Gia clumsily reached for Eva's purse. Eva, snapping to attention, easily avoided her lunge, taking Gia's head in her hands and slamming it against the wall.

"You let him take me into that room," Eva growled, holding Gia's hair in a firm grip as Gia winced. "You smiled as he took me in there. I could hear you laughing."

Gia blinked rapidly, trying to break away from Eva's grasp. "You want to call daddy now? After you got your fun in and everyone else got what was coming to them?" Eva slammed Gia's head against the wall again, as Gia let out a little shriek and crumbled to the floor.

"Eva," Leigh said quickly, pulling Eva from the room and closing the door behind them. Feeling the lock click into place, she turned to Eva, who was shaking visibly from the confrontation. "Just relax, deep breaths," she cooed, trying to calm her.

It took a few minutes for Gia to realize she had been locked in a room with several dead bodies, including Joy's. They could hear her muffled screams as she pounded on the door. Leigh nodded in the other direction, and they retreated out of the store room and into the narrow hallway.

"There's got to be an office around here somewhere," Leigh said, glancing at the hallway's locked doors. Eva nodded, trying the doors with the key card Leigh got from Danny.

"None of these work!" she cried, frustrated.

"Here!" Leigh pulled Jiménez's key card out. "Maybe his will work." After trying several more doors, they finally hit pay dirt. Eva let out a little scream of triumph as one of the doors opened with a green light and a click.

After walking down a short hallway, the room opened up into what appeared to be a meticulously kept office. This definitely belonged to Jiménez. There were various plaques on the wall with his picture. There were also a few white packages on the desk. Some were opened, with bits of white powder sprinkled on the mahogany surface.

It didn't take long to find a safe, but they quickly gave up on the elaborate combination. Turning to the desk, they had better luck. It was unlocked, revealing yet more white packets and several stacks of U.S. and Mexican money.

"Do you have room in your bag?" Leigh asked.

Eva smiled.

"I always make room for cash."

After cleaning out the stash into Eva's emptied bag, they turned their attention to the glimmering laptop on his desk. Which, coincidentally, was not password protected.

"Arrogant bastard," Leigh sniffed. Eyeing the awards on the wall, something Jiménez said jogged her memory.

"Can you look up who owns the Sol II?" Leigh asked. Eva eyed her warily.

"Why?"

"Something Jiménez said. If these fucks are really linked to some cartel, all the sister resorts must be too. And I'll also bet you this." Leigh was shaking her finger now, on a roll. Eva let her eyes drift heavenward.

"That was the boss calling them, and I think I know his name." Leigh felt her stomach tighten, and then became frustrated at her reaction, trying to push it away. "Jiménez mentioned the name, Guero. If he is the boss, he would want to stay close to his resorts."

"What do you mean?" Eva asked, forehead wrinkling.

"If you were responsible for running the resorts to launder dirty money for the cartel," Leigh surmised, trying to put the pieces together in her mind, "wouldn't you stay close to them?" Eva didn't respond, instead devoting herself to the Internet search. After a few clicks, she found their answer.

"La Playa, it's a resort in Merida under the same hotel chain. It's brand new, 5 stars, won some sort of international award. The resort group is owned by this guy, Mr. Gallegos. Nickname is Guero."

"Guero?"

"Isn't that the name Jiménez told you? Says here it's a local nickname, it means 'white boy' I know that much. It must be sarcastic because . . . well, look at him. Here."

Eva scrolled down the page to a squat man smiling broadly, flanked by women in very little clothing and what looked to be a few local politicians. Their faces reflected the excitement of a grand opening.

The majority of the faces were staring up as a group. But Leigh noticed one man standing off to the side, as if realizing the photo opportunity was a mistake. As if he did not want to be photographed. Like the other men, he wore a black suit, which complemented his complexion and dark sunglasses. Unlike the rest of the men, his hair was strikingly blonde.

"That's him, that's Guero."

"But it says here the owner," Eva tapped on the fat man in the front, "is Guero."

"No, it's him. I know it," Leigh responded, confident. Eva pursed her lips, typing on the keyboard for another search.

"Los Muertos," she announced, pointing to the screen. "This is what we are dealing with Leigh, in case you were in doubt." The images she was pointing to were sickening, until Leigh realized they had just witnessed a real-life replica down the hall.

"What is that?"

"The name of the cartel that Guero is associated with. This is the kind of people they are, Leigh. I hope you realize this."

"How far is Merida from here?" Leigh offered, changing courses, shaking the images from her mind.

"Not far, two hours or so? I was talking to the concierge about it earlier. Some of the hotel staff lives there."

"Guero must be elsewhere."

"How do you know?" Eva sounded tired trying to keep up Leigh's quick movements.

"If he was close he wouldn't have bothered talking, he'd be here by now. No, he's not close, he's far away. And he's frustrated." This seemed to wake Eva up.

"How do you know he didn't send someone here, that he isn't on his way now? And why would we go to the La Playa if that's one of his resorts, shouldn't we get as far away as possible?" The panic in Eva's voice was palpable. Leigh fended it off.

"Who would he send? His men are here, dead, in the backroom. Plus, it's embarrassing. Sending his henchmen to come kill a bunch of coed assassins in his resort?" Leigh paused to see Eva still unmoving, unconvinced. She continued.

"As far as La Playa goes, we'd be hiding in plain sight. He'd never think to look there. They will expect us to run."

Eva slowly began nodding at the logic. Leigh, assuming the conversation was over, turned and began walking towards the door. She realized a few feet away from it that Eva had not followed suit. Still situated at the desk, Eva looked directly at her before speaking.

"Did you . . . " Eva stopped herself before finishing the question, staring back at the screen before falling silent. She cleared the browser and search history. Leigh, anxious to be going, didn't allow her to finish the thought.

"Do you think you can find the person who told you earlier about Merida?"

"Yeah, he told me to come get a drink with him if I was interested . . . I wasn't."

"Go see if he's working. If he's there, ask him to take us on a day trip to Merida. Only we want to leave today, now." Leigh shifted her purse to one side, the gun she had stashed in it earlier digging into her hip.

"What are you going to do?" Eva replied, rising to follow suit.

"I'm going to figure out what to do with Joy."

Eva, who had been halfway out the door into the dark corridor, turned back to Leigh.

"Let's just leave her here."

"We can't take the chance." Leigh shook her head, preparing to depart in the opposite direction. "They might identify her, her parents will fly down. No, it's a nightmare. It's best she's never found."

"What are we going to tell everyone?" Eva wondered aloud, her voice echoing eerily as she proceeded down the hallway.

"I'm working on it."

"Tell me when you figure it out." Eva gave her a half smile and then disappeared, taking the key card with her.

8

Blessedly, Benicio was still on his shift at the concierge desk. Despite her attempt at cleaning herself up, Eva must have looked a bit frazzled, drunk even, because his smile widened as she approached.

"So, you gonna take me up on that drink?" he asked as she walked up. Eva simpered, putting one finger on her upper lip.

"Mmmmm, sure. But not here."

"Where?"

"You're going home tonight?"

Benicio started laughing, clutching his belt in a way that made her stomach twist. She had a feeling that reaction would continue for the rest of her life.

"You mean home, as in Merida?"

"Yes, Merida!" Eva fairly squeaked. "All the girls want to go!"

"You all want to go!" Benicio's brown eyes got wider, his straight white teeth gleamed under his small moustache. This was pathetically easy, Eva thought, before continuing her rehearsed story.

"All except Joy—she's staying down here with a guy she met," Eva said.

"What guy?" Benicio asked, throwing Eva a bit. He looked apprehensive. Eva was as flippant as possible.

"Oh, some guy, a friend of Mr. Jiménez." Eva was careful to keep her tenses in the present.

"Friends," Benicio responded, staring at her, looking confused. Eva gave a ditzy laugh and flipped her hair around, which seemed to calm him.

"We are *so* excited, are you ready?"

"I get off at 5 am."

Eva took this in, calculating the hours it had been since their night began.

"Ok, where will you bring the car?"

*

"Ready?" Eva had run back to the compound to find Leigh and the room service cart now in Jiménez's office. Leigh didn't hear Eva enter; she was busying herself with uncovering more guns. She already had five: one from the guy she killed on the patio, one from Jiménez, and three others she found in the office. They all looked frightening. She hastily began stuffing them into her bag before zipping it closed.

"I found some stuff," she said, by way of explanation.

"Benicio is pulling up the car, he thinks we're in here finishing up with Mr. Jiménez."

"Nice. Is that the guy you ran into earlier? He knows Mr. Jiménez?"

"Well, he calls him boss."

Leigh accepted this with a nod.

"I decided what we will do with Joy."

Eva glanced at Gia's weekender bag, which Leigh had placed prominently on top of the cart. It was a black and red quilted pattern, large enough to accommodate Gia's expansive wardrobe. Eva raised an eyebrow.

*

"Well, this is kind of terrifying but she fits perfectly in here." Eva strained to keep the blood splattered head away from her as they crumbled Joy's body into Gia's bag, the contents of which were scattered around the floor.

"Pick it up, and put it in there." Leigh directed at Gia, who, at gunpoint, had dutifully listened to the girls since they let her out of her temporary holding cell. Gia seemed to have reverted back to her complacent state. She absentmindedly began stuffing her now-discarded wardrobe and toiletries into a garbage bag she had found in Jiménez's office. Straining slightly, Eva and Leigh picked up Gia's weekender bag and hobbled it onto the cart with a thud.

Pink now touching the sky, the group slowly pushed the heavily laden cart down the pathway towards reception. Benicio was waiting with a dumb grin on his face. Helping them with their bags, he looked at Gia's shuffling, drawn form. As he finished packing up the car, he gave Eva an inquiring look at her catatonic state.

"She got sick. Too much tequila."

"Oh, ha!" he cried, teasing Gia as they got in the car, speeding past the gates of the Sol II and down the highway that connected Cancun to the rest of the Peninsula. As the car drifted north up towards Merida, Leigh fashioned an old sweatshirt as a makeshift pillow. Gia followed suit, seemingly collapsing upon herself in the adjoining seat. Eva stayed up and chatted with Benicio, obviously needing to talk.

The sky had lightened considerably when they arrived at the resort nearly two hours later.

"I get you a suite, on the cheap!" Benicio cried, carrying the girls' bags to the reception as they waited for him in the car.

"Leigh, shit, our passports." Eva sprung to life in the front seat, turning around to face Leigh.

"Don't worry about it," Leigh responded. "He thinks we're with Mr. Jiménez. We won't have to sign anything here."

"No, I mean we left our passports at Sol II when we checked in."

"Fuck," Leigh whined, "how could we forget our passports?" She shook off the cobwebs of sleep with growing alarm, tapping her fingers on her thigh. "Put it out of your mind for now, let's just focus on staying safe. We can work out how to get them back later." Not quite satisfied with this, but too tired to argue, Eva slumped back into the car seat.

By this time, Gia had woken, letting out a small whimper and looking out at the resort with a vacant gaze. Leigh noticed a trail of blood trickling from her nose.

"Geez Eva, you must have hit her hard," she whispered under her breath. Eva glanced back from the passenger seat.

"That wasn't me." It took a few seconds to realize what she meant. And as Gia slipped back to sleep, Leigh glanced down in the garbage bag which held her hastily packed garments.

There, nestled between wads of underwear and primer, was a small white packet. Leigh stared at it for a time, before her gaze wandered back to a smiling Benicio. He was walking proudly back to the car, room keys in hand.

"I cannot wait to get some sleep." Leigh sighed, feeling the strain of the last few hours.

Exhausted, the girls practically crawled into the room, which was outfitted much like the one they had just vacated. The flat screens, the generous patio—only the hot tub and outdoor bar were missing. They put Gia in a bed by herself and took the adjoining bedroom. Leigh was asleep before her head hit the pillow. Before she dropped off, she vaguely felt Eva moving around, restless.

*

When Leigh woke up, it was just past noon. A line of light under the bathroom door first drew her attention. As she spotted Eva out on the balcony, it didn't take much to guess who was in there.

"What are you doing?" Leigh asked, swinging the bathroom door open. Gia attempted to get up, caught her foot in her black dress, and fell over to one side. Bits of white power flitted to the ground, and the duct-taped packet was sitting like an accusation at her side. She started shaking, eyes darting around, breathing fast and quick.

Leigh surveyed the scene, left the tiny pile on the tiled floor, and took the packet with her, closing the door as if on a family pet. Looking for a handy hiding place, she stowed the packet neatly in the decorative alcove in the living room. It couldn't be kept from Gia long, but it would probably buy her a few hours of frantic searching. She was still on her tip-toes when Eva walked in from the patio.

"Where's Gia?"

"In the bathroom, snorting something. I hid the packet up here." Leigh waved above her head as she jumped down from the coffee table she had pushed up against the wall. Eva looked unsettled. Leigh watched the range of emotions flow across her face, as she struggled to get herself alert and awake. Leigh fished around for Gia's cigarettes she had stashed in the garbage bag. Eva twisted her hands together as she spoke.

"Leigh, we didn't just forget our passports—we forgot about Danny."

"Who?" Leigh lit the cigarette and took a long, grateful drag.

"Danny, the guy who we had dinner with last night. The guy that went looking for you. Pockmarked face, ponytail." Despite the relaxing effect of the cigarette, Leigh felt her stomach tighten. A vision of Danny speaking in concerned tones while she hid, inebriated, on the beach sprung to her mind.

"How the fuck did we elude him?"

"Call it luck, we were all over that place. In Jiménez's office . . . ."

"He was probably watching us."

"Shit," Eva confirmed.

"Has Benicio left yet?" Leigh inquired, tapping the cigarette into an ashtray.

"No, he's still here."

"You haven't slept."

Eva didn't respond, just gazed off in the direction of the patio, looking anxious.

"We have to go back," Leigh stated, taking another pull from her cigarette. "There's the passport situation for one. And we have to take care of Danny."

"We can't," whispered Eva, "we're safe here."

"Safe? You must be joking. They surely know Benicio, they'll ask around, and he'll tell them."

"What's your solution Leigh?" Eva snapped back, her liquid black eyes quivering.

"Well, we're not going back with the sun still up." Leigh placed her unevenly tan leg in front of her and frowned. "Let's go to the pool."

*

They sat, baking in the sun, next to an overcrowded pool that glittered an unnatural blue. The pair was going on their third margarita when Eva looked directly at Leigh.

"What happened?"

"You mean last night?" Leigh responded, definitely buzzed.

"Yes."

"Well, I killed a bunch of people and now we're on the run from a drug cartel." Leigh tipped the drink back to get the last of the frozen cocktail.

"Would you keep your voice down," Eva shot back, adjusting her sunglasses and looking around warily. "I meant in the room

61

Leigh," Eva continued, whispering, eyeing the oblivious pool guests with suspicion. "Tell me what happened."

"I told you, Jiménez shot Joy, so I shot him."

Eva crossed her arms, looking upset. Leigh responded by putting on more suntan oil and hastily flipping to her stomach. She let herself drift into a light sleep, her mind running from the fact that Joy was still stuffed inside a quilted bag she had purchased with Gia at Scottsdale Fashion Park. Even though she was distinctly aware she was at a pool, on a lounge chair, in Mexico, she slowly felt reality drift away into a dream.

Leigh knew she was dreaming, but she continued walking up to a ranch house in what appeared to be the desert. She had the impression she was supposed to go in. It was late in the day, and as she looked around her, she spotted one of those beautiful sunsets that makes one forget about the heat. Slowly, she entered the house, closing the door behind her.

Leigh paused for a moment, finding herself in a low-lit foyer with the traditional terracotta tans and white of southwestern houses. She moved through a narrow hallway lined with Kachina dolls, quickening her pace as she passed their colorful outfits and menacing faces. The hallway exited into a dimly lit great room. Here, she paused, feeling something move in the shadows behind her. Her heart was thumping out of her chest with anticipation. She heard footsteps, and closed her eyes.

*

"Do you want another one?" the waiter beckoned, looking down at her with a gleaming, white smile.

"Uh, I'm fine thanks," Leigh murmured, shaking sleep away and looking around her. Eva had left, there was only a crumpled towel lying on the chair next to hers.

When she returned to their suite, dropping her bag and suntan oil on the chair, Eva was waiting for her. If Eva had a buzz, it had completely worn off. Leigh, though she had slept through that morning, felt tiredness creeping in. She stretched her limbs with a grunt, anticipating what Eva's next words would be.

"Leigh, we can't go back," Eva stated, looking at Leigh nervously. For a moment, Leigh wondered if she was hitting the same substance Gia had stashed away. She only belatedly realized Eva was reacting in a practically normal, rational manner. The only one of them who was.

"I know you don't want to," Leigh began, sitting down on the couch across from her friend. "But we need those passports back, and we need to . . . take care of Danny. Before he finds us."

Eva scowled, pacing the room.

"We aren't vigilantes, Leigh. Danny will kill us on sight, we should make a run for it."

Instead of arguing, Leigh caught sight of the quilted bag, positioned under a stack of towels in the kitchen.

"Ok," she replied, watching Eva relax slightly. She continued, "But have you thought we might be getting ahead of ourselves?"

Eva looked at her, and then immediately at the bag.

"Oh," she said, almost surprised.

"Exactly," Leigh responded. "First things first. We need to get rid of the body."

9

On the way to the reception area, they compared notes. Benicio had the weekend off. He would show them around for what remained of the day, and would then go home to his village near Merida.

"Cenotes!" exclaimed Leigh, as they found him sitting behind the reception area in a place employees could come and socialize. By the look of the empty bottles in the garbage can, Benicio had enjoyed several beverages in anticipation for the outing.

"We really want to see a cenote," echoed Eva, looking at Benicio and smiling.

"I know the best cenote, it's near Cenotillo!" he drawled, mixing English and Spanish as he grew more excited. A date alone with two beautiful ladies?

"Sounds great, when can we leave?"

"They are most beautiful at sunset," he responded, raising his eyes suggestively at Eva. Leigh cracked a grin.

"Before we go, would you mind bringing your car around to our room? I have a bag I want to take with me."

They locked Gia in the bathroom by building a mini barricade outside the door. But by that time, she was so doped up she was barely capable of stopping the drool from rolling down her mouth. They left her some snacks from the mini bar and departed, decked out in tiny bathing suits and the most garish wraps they could find. Eva and Leigh hauled the most important piece of luggage together.

"This doesn't even cover anything," Eva complained, struggling to both hold her end of the bag and pull the edges of the bikini top down. It had its desired effect, Benicio seemed hypnotized.

Leigh had borrowed one of Gia's outfits—a flowing maxi dress over her own black bikini. The heat and humidity, even at this hour, was too intense for so much coverage. But the length of the dress and the empire waist neatly covered the gun she had secured around her waist with one of Gia's belts.

Once on the road, the feel of the metal against Leigh's skin was oddly calming as she watched the scenery whizz past. Benicio and Eva were talking in low voices, the heat of the day and their measured tones made Leigh almost drop off to sleep again when the car abruptly came to a halt.

Leigh glanced out at what looked like a tangle of green jungle. It wasn't until she hopped out of the car and advanced a few steps that the large sinkhole came into focus, nearly half a football field in length. It looked deep, and as she advanced towards the opening her heart skipped a beat as she glanced into the darkness below. She pulled out her cellphone and deftly tracked the GPS coordinates. Turning, she walked back to the car, just as Benicio went to grab the duffel bag from the trunk.

"It's heavy," he said suddenly, dropping the lumpy bag to the ground with a thump.

"Gear for if we decide to dive later," responded Leigh.

"I can do it!" Benicio said dramatically. He flexed his biceps, picked up the bag, and walked them towards the cenote. A small crowd of tourists were being led around the rim, and Eva and Leigh slowly made their way to the entrance.

"Drop it here. I'm going to rest for a second." Leigh found a handy rock right near the edge of the opening and settled herself down, thanking the Mexican government for not believing in guard rails.

"You guys go on." She flipped her hand to shoo them away, a smile on her face. Eva pried away Benicio's hand from the bag, which was now placed next to Leigh. Gamely, Eva led him down the path to view the stunning sunset. Leigh sat and watched them go, sensing the bag near her feet.

When the tourists were gazing at the surrounding waterfalls, and the light was just right, Leigh nudged the bag from its precarious grip on the ledge. The last she saw of Joy was a slip of quilted red and black as it tumbled into the darkness. She didn't even hear the splash when it hit the water.

When Benicio and Eva returned, they were talking in hushed tones and looking conspiratorial. For a brief second, Leigh felt her stomach tighten. Did Eva give them away? Eva must have picked up on Leigh's thoughts, and as she passed her friend she gave her a small pinch.

"I'm going to stay with Benicio tonight."

"Ok," Leigh responded, still feeling uneasy.

"He is going to help us," Eva whispered, as they followed him back to the car. Leigh nodded, feeling much like she did the night before, when she walked into the room to find Joy and Jiménez entwined.

They left Leigh at their suite at the La Playa, and Eva squeezed her hand before they sped away. Still with a sense of unease, Leigh went to the bar to have some dinner. After fending off the attentions of the bartender and a pack of Australians, she returned to the room, removed the barricade and checked on Gia.

"You have to shower at some point," she said, discovering Gia in the same place they had left her. Gia didn't look as if she moved an inch. The food was eaten though. Gia shook her head and brought her knees to her chest.

"Come watch TV, Gia," Leigh offered, pulling her by the hand and placing her in front of the TV. It was some Mexican game show where people were sticking themselves to a Velcro wall. The show was followed by the nightly news.

No story about a room full of decapitated Mexican drug lords, or missing American girls for that matter. Further evidence that what Jiménez said was right, Leigh surmised. They were the police.

Leaving Gia to stare glassy-eyed at the television, Leigh went back into the master suite with every intention of thinking things through. Instead, she fell asleep.

*

A ringing phone woke her and she glanced at the nightstand clock—it was just after 6 am. It took a few seconds to remember which phone was which, but Leigh grabbed Jiménez's phone and accepted the call.

"Nice work," said the voice on the other end of the phone. Leigh's heart was pounding; she felt a trickle of bile move into her throat.

"I hear you lost your friend though, that's really too bad. You should be thinking of them before you took such rash actions."

So then Danny must have stuck around long enough to somehow get wind of Joy's death. Leigh wondered what else he saw. She swore silently, holding the phone closely and planning her next move.

"You only have your thugs to blame, Guero," she began, rubbing the sleep from her eyes. "Looks like they picked the wrong girls to invite to dinner."

There was no answer for a few seconds. Apparently, calling him out by name threw him for a moment. Leigh realized she had a knack for doing that, and it certainly seemed to be a new sensation for him.

"It doesn't matter. Jiménez got what was coming to him. You actually did me a favor."

"Did I?"

"You found the bodies, didn't you? Stealing from me is a bad idea. Jiménez and his men learned this the hard way. Danny was in the middle of taking care of them. He was supposed to finish off your friends in the condo after that job was complete. You must be a ghost, because he never found you."

"He never came back to finish anyone off," Leigh shot back, wondering if in her rush of adrenaline they were being watched the entire time. Was he standing on the patio? Did this man have eyes everywhere?

The conversation paused, and Leigh felt slightly unnerved by how easily her conversation with a cartel kingpin was going. She also felt a strange urgency, as if she was concerned the phone call might soon be over. That the conversation would stop. Fuck. This was confusing.

"You'll have to turn yourselves in, this has gone far enough." His tone was convincing, like a good friend coaxing another friend off the ledge. The problem was, Leigh always intended to be pushed.

"Sorry, I can't let that happen." She lifted herself slightly, putting her head in her hand and yawning. Her equally cool tone seemed to anger him, and the next words were tight and dark.

"Not only is your friend dead, you've stumbled on something I wasn't quite finished with, you see? You are a loose end, and in my business that is a liability."

Leigh got the sense that he had told her far too much, and that only happened when one person seriously underestimated the other. She felt herself getting angry. He was genuinely trying to reason with her, encouraging her to turn them all in so he could what—kill them once they did?

"I told you what I wanted," she replied. Now he paused.

"Money is no use when you are dead, which is what you will be if you continue. My superiors aren't as accommodating as I am."

"Oh really," Leigh began, in her best condescending tone. "If Danny did his job I wouldn't be talking to you. He probably got a good look at what I did to his little friend on a patio and took off. He won't be so lucky the next time I see him." Leigh knew how obnoxious and insignificant she must sound to him. She would show him. Besides, who the hell did he think he was? She decided to show off a bit.

"And let me remind you in case you are in any doubt as to what a lot of fucking money is, it's 5 million with an escort to the border." There was no answer on the phone. Leigh glanced down to make sure they hadn't been disconnected. Guero finally spoke, without the patronizing tone he had used earlier.

"All I can tell you is to turn yourself in and we'll come to an agreement. You keep going on like this, and I can't promise anything. Right now you're my little problem. If I were you, I'd keep it that way. I'm a reasonable man, to a point."

"You've given me little incentive to turn ourselves in."

"You'll escape with your lives," he responded, hinting at letting them live for the first time. He paused. "As I said before, I think we should meet, to discuss this in more detail."

Leigh quickly hung up the phone, her heart beating. Her knowledge of phone tracing methods was crude, at best, educated primarily from bad action movies. That aside, she had the feeling that he was closing in on their location. She called Eva.

"We need to leave."

"I know. We're coming to get you. Bring everything with you. We'll be there in an hour."

Leigh took her time showering and attending to her hair and makeup, not knowing when she might have access to hot water again. Gia had migrated to the living room. Still watching TV, she looked like she had showered, and was snacking on some chips from the minibar.

"We're leaving Gia, get up."

Gia dutifully followed, lugging her garbage bag back with her.

"Where's Joy?" Gia asked, with a particularly vacant look. Leigh ignored the question.

"Here." Leigh retrieved the packet from above the alcove and shoved it at Gia. Gia's eyes wavered, and then settled on the tiny slit of white the duct tape failed to cover. Watching her taste just a little, Leigh took it back and placed it in her bag.

Dragging their bags to reception, they were greeted by Benicio's rusted out car. He helped them load their bags, looking pleased with himself, Leigh immediately grew suspicious.

"What did you tell him," she hissed at Eva, who shushed her from the passenger seat. Leigh slid over in the back, allowing Gia to climb in next to her. In a matter of minutes they were deep in the lush foliage of Merida. As Gia stared blankly out the window, Leigh tried to keep track of where they were going, quickly losing her sense of direction.

After a half hour or so, they finally pulled into a nondescript row of small structures that were practically shacks. Away from this cluster, there were several sturdy looking structures that looked well maintained—their subtle colors making them appear to melt into the surrounding foliage.

"Welcome to my home," Benicio said, as they exited the car, following him toward one of the smaller houses.

He lived with his mother, an older woman with a sun baked face, who promptly sat them all down and fed them. Gia picked at her food while Leigh and Eva listened to Benicio extol the benefits of living in his village. After Benicio left the table to assist his mother in the garden, Leigh turned to Eva.

"So, the story is this," Eva said, feeling Leigh's discomfort. "We are here on vacation and we want to make money by running drugs."

If Leigh's mouth was capable of dropping, it would have now.

"*What* did you tell him?" Leigh asked in a low voice, snapping out the words for emphasis.

"That we're broke! That we didn't tell our parents we're down here, and now we ran out of money," Eva paused, a devilish grin appearing on her face. "Let's just say he realized how desperate I was last night." Eva winked at Leigh, which elicited a snort response from Gia. Both girls ignored her.

"We need something else though," Leigh said. "Tell him we have to convince our recruiters that we're serious. We need to know how to shoot, big guns."

"I'm one step ahead of you," Eva responded, taking a sip of beer and smiling. "Benicio has connections, he's in charge of hiding weapons caches for his cartel."

"Which is?" Leigh queried, phone at the ready.

"Los Muertos," Eva supplied, taking another long sip.

"Ah ha, a familiar name," Leigh replied, doing a cursory search with whatever information she could find on her phone.

"What?" Eva asked, beer momentarily forgotten.

"You forget, it's the same cartel that has been linked to, you-know-who, Guero."

"Just how high up the chain is this guy, Guero?"

"I guess we can ask your new boyfriend," Leigh said flippantly. This time Eva did not smile back.

"This is a fine line we are walking, Leigh."

"You are the one who came up with this ridiculous story," Leigh shot back. Before she could continue, Benicio rejoined them. As he lowered himself to the table, Eva whispered a few words to him. He gave a wide grin, but then noticed Gia staring at them and gave a frown.

"She's on something. Leave her here. My mom will watch her." They again parked Gia in front of the TV, and Leigh followed Eva and Benicio to a small building in the back of the house.

The security was very sophisticated, which made Leigh nervous for the first time since their bizarre journey began. The river of cash the cartel was generating was obviously being poured directly into preserving its assets. When Benicio pressed his thumb then retina to the scanning device, Leigh felt her limbs tingle. This was serious business.

Inside, there was a gated entryway, and beyond that, darkness. Benicio flipped on the lights, smiling at Eva as he showed off his exclusive access. Leigh left them near the entrance and walked down the narrow hallway, proceeding cautiously. As she got a glimpse of the weapons cache, she knew why Eva sounded so confident.

"Is that . . . a flame thrower?" Leigh asked, staring in disbelief at the mounted object as Benicio and Eva joined her. Benicio began laughing and Eva gave her a nervous glance.

"Which ones do we try?" Eva asked, twirling the strap of her top into little knots.

"The scariest ones," Leigh responded. "We try the scariest fucking ones."

10

As they loaded semi-automatic weapons and bags of clips into supplied duffle bags, Leigh studied the arsenal.

"Benicio, we need another favor. Can we borrow your car?"

"You want more help?" he exclaimed, now beginning to look a bit hesitant. He narrowed his eyes, thinking through their story with a hint of suspicion.

"You say someone is going to show you the ropes?"

"That's right; this guy named Danny," Leigh responded. Eva raised an eyebrow at the name, and Leigh realized she had yet to fill her in on her conversation with Guero. She attempted to inform both audiences.

"Yep. He's our recruiter. We met him at the resort when we arrived," Leigh continued.

"If I know Danny," Benicio began, winking at the girls with a knowing grin. Both Leigh and Eva shifted visibly. So then it was true, Benicio and Danny knew each other because they both worked for Los Muertos. Which meant they both worked for Guero. Benicio, oblivious to their growing anxiety, continued, "He's going to get a hard on seeing you guys; he'll hire you on the spot."

"That's what we're hoping," said Leigh, who began to seriously doubt the intellect of their new friend.

After they brought the haul out of the compound, locks clicking behind them, Leigh turned to Eva. "So is he going to loan us his car?"

"I think he will. Just for tonight, he has to be at work tomorrow," Eva whispered, glancing backwards at Benicio, who was securing the door to the compound.

"So he can stay here all night and watch Gia?"

"Yes. What exactly are we planning Leigh?"

"Our passports are back at the Sol II resort, yes? There's also the matter of Danny."

Benicio gave out a call and began directing them to the back of the building they just exited.

"You have to learn to shoot these things," Benicio muttered, leading the way to a path through the dense foliage. Letting him take the lead a comfortable space in front of them, Eva picked up their previous conversation.

"If you are asking if I want to get our passports and then drive like hell for the border, then yes. But why are we telling him we are looking for Danny?" She swatted a bit of green vine which had gotten tangled in her skirt, threatening to wrap her up in the folds of the jungle. Leigh helped her free the garment.

"Because Danny is looking for us. Guero made that clear. We might as well find him first."

"And when we find him, after we get our passports back that is, what do we do?"

"Improvise?" Leigh lied, knowing full well what her plan of action would be when she found Danny. "Unless you were being serious back there about wanting to join up with the cartel."

"It was just a story to get him to help us," a disgusted Eva responded back.

Leigh paused in the jungle path, feeling the humidity wrap tightly against her limbs. The environment was thick with heat, both of them were exhausted. Leigh stared at her friend, who was decidedly looking the other way, off into the dense green of their surroundings. She turned and began walking. "Come on, let's go learn how to shoot these fucking things."

As Benicio took them deeper into the jungle, the heat was now so intense that Leigh felt her pulse thud with every step. Leigh could hear Benicio's voice drifting ahead of her. He was talking about his boss, Guero. Apparently, this was where he liked to do target practice.

"So what's he like?" Leigh asked once they reached the range, loading the clip with a satisfying smack and taking aim at the rock bluffs in front of her.

"Guero? A business man, a good boss. Tough, but fair," Benicio responded, picking up a gun himself and expertly inserting the clip. "Good to his staff."

"What if his staff isn't good to him?" Eva asked, situated next to Leigh. She let go a staccato of bullets that pinged off the rocks.

"Have you shot before?" Benicio asked.

"I grew up in Arizona, of course I have." She smiled and Leigh laughed. Benicio accepted this response, and crinkled his forehead, pondering Eva's earlier question.

"Those who aren't good to him go missing. Turn up without their heads . . . " He would have continued, but Leigh let off a satisfying rain of bullets.

"This is easy."

"I know," said Eva. After Benicio brought out tequila and lined up some bottles for them to practice on, the shooting became more erratic. He loaded a semi-automatic for Leigh, who started shooting in bursts at the targets.

"Fuck, this is hard to control."

"Wicked kickback," Eva acknowledged, taking a long drink from the bottle.

"Ok, one more." Leigh knocked the target off its ledge, sending the glass bottle spinning gracefully in the air. It fell with a shatter. Benicio raised his hands in triumph and Eva clapped for Leigh, who did a mock curtsey in response. They settled down to watch the sunset, and after Benicio regaled them with more tales of the cartel, Leigh eventually steered him back to the subject of Guero.

"He owns the hotels," Benicio began, "but runs them as part of the cartel's business. Not to say he won't kill you. He will, but he's more . . . meaningful about it."

Leigh nodded, as if that made any sense.

Before heading back to Benicio's house for a brief respite, Leigh typed "Guero" into her smartphone for a quick Internet search. Her heart leapt when pictures came onto the screen. It wasn't the short fat man they had found on the resort's website but was, in fact, the man she had seen standing off to the side.

She scrolled down a few pages. He had been in and out of jail, all for unrelated charges because they couldn't seem to nail him on anything directly related to cartel activity. She put the phone down, feeling it burn slightly in her hand. This was crazy, he was most likely out to kill her and she was becoming infatuated. It had to stop. Putting the phone firmly away, she followed Eva and Benicio back to the house.

"I'm going to rest a bit," Leigh said, "let's leave around 8 pm?"

"Ok," Eva responded. She was helping Benicio's mom in the tiny kitchen, attempting to speak in broken Spanish. Leigh walked in to the living room to find Gia still sitting in front of the TV, not bothering to remove the smudges of white around her nostrils. Collapsing on the opposite couch, Leigh closed her eyes.

*

Leigh was walking around campus. The sun was blinding, so bright she could hardly see in front of her. She was walking fast but she didn't seem to be going anywhere. One thought paralyzed her.

I'm going to miss class.

Up ahead, she noticed a tree in front of her lecture hall. The shade looked wonderful, especially on such a hot, sunny day. Shade was at a premium in their climate, and she was glad to take advantage of it. It wasn't until Leigh was under the tree that she noticed a woman to her right, sitting quietly underneath. She had fine features and long, dark hair, which she swished to the side so it didn't fall into the book she was reading.

"Hot out," Leigh said by way of conversation, looking at the door to her lecture hall like it was a million miles away. The girl didn't respond but looked up, smiled, and then continued reading her book. Leigh settled down next to her.

Now level with her companion, she felt the breeze come across her brow and could almost see the heat rise from off the pavement. She looked over at what the girl was reading, but couldn't make much out of it. After some time, Leigh looked again at the girl. Slowly, she stood up.

"Rachel?"

*

Leigh's eyes flew open to see Gia slumped on the couch. She eyed her watch—7:45 pm. Sitting up, she shook off the dream and went to get Eva. It was time to find Danny.

11

Leigh settled into the passenger seat with her phone attuned to the GPS navigation. They drove the nearly two hour trip in silence. A few minutes away from their destination, Eva broke the quiet.

"I was talking to Benicio more. About the cartel."

Leigh didn't respond. Partly from not knowing what to say, and partly waiting to see if Eva's edgy mood would shortly be explained. She had been short with Leigh soon after Leigh woke from her nap.

"He said the last person to steal from the cartel was shipped in a cooler to the local sheriff. In a cooler. The rest of him was never found. Because you see, they mailed him in parts. There was blood. Which meant they had cut him apart while he was still alive."

"Am I doing this by myself?"

"No, Leigh, but why are we doing this in the first place? Let's make a break for the border. We have some cash, we certainly have the firepower. Let's just go and get out of here. Screw the 5 mil."

"And say what Eva? What do we say? Gia's still back at Benicio's—how do we explain to her dad that we left his little girl in some shack in Mexico? What about Joy's parents? What about ours? Do you think they'd ever believe us about the cartels and the resort? It's not possible."

"This is suicide," Eva shot back. "I might have been in shock earlier, but I'm awake now Leigh. And I know you're holding something back."

"What are you talking about?"

"How did Joy get shot? You never told me what went on in there. You haven't told me what you said to Guero, or . . . "

"The less I tell you, the better. If no one knows about you, they can't use you against me."

"You think you're protecting me?" Eva laughed. "Leigh they don't care. They'll kill us both in a heartbeat." Leigh could see Eva clenching the wheel to steady her shaking hands.

"I didn't want to drag you into this, but I had to. I had to get you away from him and once I did, I couldn't leave you there."

"I know you wouldn't have left me," replied Eva, frustrated. "But you aren't listening; we don't have to do this. We didn't have to do any of this. We can go to the police . . . "

"There are no FUCKING POLICE!" Leigh shouted, letting her own frustrations boil over. "Doesn't anything we've been through prove that to you? Where was the newscast about our disappearance, Eva, or the pile of bodies in the hotel? Where are the police? They are the police; these people own them. We need to make a deal with Guero. It's our best way out of here."

"This has gotten way out of hand, Leigh, and we're bringing other unwanted attention. How do you know that Guero is the only one with his hands in this mess? Benicio tells me his cartel is in some serious turf war with some other cartel called La Familia. We might be jumping from the frying pan into the fire."

"Guero can help us get out, if I can convince him to," Leigh responded, knowing she was being unreasonably stubborn, but truly believing her gut instinct.

"You hardly know this person Leigh!" Eva cried in frustration.

"I just know it Eva," Leigh responded confidently. After she spoke they sat in silence, the highway now shrouded in darkness.

Driving up to the entrance to Sol II, Eva found a parking space not far from the lobby. The two stepped out of the car and adjusted their clothing, leaving behind their unfinished argument for the time being.

"I would lift up the skirt a bit," Leigh offered, applying a new layer of lipstick.

"Well you certainly can't lift yours up any more—your ass is practically hanging out," Eva responded.

"It's Gia's," Leigh smirked, adjusting the tight black dress as much as the hemline would allow. She hoped they looked like a bunch of ditzy American tourists. As they entered the resort, the glances they received confirmed this assumption.

"Do you think we'll be recognized?" Eva asked, confidence wavering.

"No, there are plenty of women here who look just like us," Leigh responded, guiding her to the reception area.

"Do we get the passports first?" Eva asked, pausing.

"Let's get a round, then the passports." Leigh changed direction, walking them to the hotel bar.

"And then what?"

"Then I need to steal something we should have taken the first time. Something that we can use as leverage," Leigh replied. They were almost to the bar, sounds of loud conversation and music greeting them.

"I'm trusting you Leigh, don't let me down," Eva said quietly as they took their seats.

"I know," Leigh said in a light tone, not wanting to draw attention. After the bartender came over and they ordered a round of shots, she turned back to Eva.

"It looks pretty normal."

Leigh was amazed at the nonchalance of the place. Nothing had changed! These people didn't all work for the cartel! They all seemed so happy, so oblivious. After the first round, however, Leigh soon felt a sinking feeling that this was not entirely true. The bartenders looked friendly but were also holding the girls' gazes for longer, their expressions altered with a hardened look. They were looking for someone.

Leigh also noticed more men in dark suits wandering the resort, seemingly inquiring as to everyone's good time. Leigh felt the flood of alcohol in her system.

"Let's go." She locked arms with Eva, and as they walked toward the reception area she slightly dug her nails into the inside of Eva's arm. The lobby was crawling with stern looking men. She paused in the pathway just yards from the entrance, not wanting to draw attention to their hesitancy, but desperately wanting to run very far away.

But their pause had been noticed, they had been spotted. A very large, beefy man began walking towards them. Instinctively, Leigh whirled around. Quick to intercept, Eva grabbed her around the waist and pretended to hold her up.

As the man drew closer, Eva nuzzled her friend and let out a dramatic giggle. Leigh played along, grabbing Eva and kissing her firmly. This stopped the man in his tracks. He pulled at his collar with a smile, and quickly diverted his attention to a pack of women doing body shots at the bar. Leigh, not exactly feigning tipsiness, watched him walk off with relief.

"I guess we go to plan b, steal something," Eva whispered sarcastically. "Remind me Leigh, what are we stealing again?"

"It's back near Jiménez's office," Leigh said in a low voice.

Arms linked, they made their way down the winding path to the private dining room they had inhabited only a few nights before.

"We can't just go walking in," Eva whispered.

"We follow the coastline," Leigh responded, pulling her quickly towards that direction. "This is how I got back to the room the first time."

As they made their way down to the beach, the salty air and crashing waves greeted them like old friends. Soon, they happened on a familiar sight.

"See, there," Leigh cried. Past landscaping designed to keep tourists at bay, they easily walked down past Jiménez's private dining area and patio. Leigh stopped in front of the object that had jogged her memory.

The boat rocked back and forth with the waves, sleek as a cigarette, almost disappearing into the blackness of the night.

"I remember that boat," Eva had joined her, whispering needlessly, as the beach was deserted.

"Come on, we might as well do this while the coast is clear." Together they made their way up the beach and past the patio, following the winding path to the building behind it.

As the two quickened their step, Leigh pulled the electronic key card from her purse. They entered, arriving in the same cavernous hallway from the previous night. Slipping off their heels, they waited.

Leigh could hear Eva's controlled breathing, and just as Leigh was about to lead them to the storage room, they heard a faint door slam somewhere inside. Quickly, Leigh pulled Eva in the adjacent bathroom she had found the night of the dinner, pulling the door behind them and leaving it open a crack. She held it there just in time to see Danny exit the door to the storage room.

The light illuminated Danny's pockmarked face for a brief moment, and as the door shut behind him, they were once again shrouded in darkness. Leigh traced the sounds of his footsteps down the hall before hearing the door to the compound swing shut. It was a few minutes before either of them spoke.

"Do you think anyone else is in there?"

"If we find someone, we'll just act drunk."

"Are you kidding? They are looking for us—they'll shoot on the spot."

"We can always go back."

"Why? This is what we came for." Eva seemed to acknowledge the true purpose of the night's mission. There had been no mention of going back to get those passports. It was too dangerous.

"Are you ready?" Leigh asked, into the darkness of the bathroom. She heard Eva exhale slowly.

"Let's go," she responded.

Leigh took the lead out of the bathroom, walking down the narrow hallway to the door of the storage room. It didn't take a rocket scientist to guess what she had intended on stealing. Leigh stood next to the door, opening it with her key card.

As the lights illuminated, empty racks of the long, narrow storage room came to light. They looked around, dumbfounded.

"I can't believe it . . . it's gone. Holy shit."

"There must have been a thousand of those packages," Eva said. Leigh felt a flood of disappointment. Putting a hand to her forehead, she saw the pieces fall together in her mind.

"I'm sorry, you trusted me."

"What?"

"I'm an idiot. They must have been moving this since we left. That's probably the job for Danny that Guero was talking about."

"Just how often are you talking to him?" Eva shot at her, seemingly more upset about her conversation with Guero then the fact that plan b was now kaput. Leigh shifted visibly, her grey eyes clearly defined by the liner they had both applied earlier. She almost looked sheepish.

"This morning," she responded, pulling her dress down a little. "He wants to meet, says it is the best way of coming to an agreement about us leaving."

"Then let's do it!" Eva cried, throwing her hands up—finally, what Eva wanted to hear.

"Eva, what we need is a guarantee."

"What we need is to be a thousand miles from here, that's what we need Leigh!" Eva's raised voice echoed in the room as she thrust her finger to the ground for emphasis.

"I was just thinking we could take it, that's all, for our own protection."

Eva rolled her eyes, her black curls falling in front of her face. Leigh looked at her friend and smiled.

"Uh oh, what. What, Leigh?" Eva said, now starting to look a little uneasy.

"Didn't you wear your hair straight the night of the dinner?"

"Um, yes, so?" Eva responded warily.

"Do you think Danny would recognize you with it curly?"

"I don't know, maybe," Eva responded, eyes narrowed. "Listen, it was dangerous enough coming back here—they are obviously looking for us. Just what are you proposing? We walk up to Danny and offer ourselves up?"

"We need to find where they put that stuff, Eva. We need collateral, it might be our only passage out of here. What if you went up to Danny and did some investigating."

"How will that work?" Eva responded, glowering, though it was halfhearted at best. Leigh took hold of her indecision.

"They think we're fucking idiots Eva," she began, looking around at the empty room. She looked at her friend, whose expression seemed to echo her thoughts. They stood in silence for a few moments.

"You want to know why I want all that money? I want these assholes to know what it feels like to get screwed over by a bunch of 'idiot' girls. I want them to regret how they've treated us."

Eva looked at her, blinking rapidly. Leigh thought about the video, how Eva must have felt when it flicked on the screen and everyone knew it was her. She thought of Gia's endless barbs. Finally, Eva spoke.

"I spotted Danny at the outdoor bar when we arrived. How much you want to bet he went back there." Now it was Leigh who blinked. So they could both keep secrets.

"Let's go then," Leigh responded, gazing at the empty racks one last time. Eva took out her compact and needlessly studied her face, giving her hair a good toss.

"Ready."

12

Danny *was* at the outdoor bar, not appearing to be on high alert. In fact, he was in the middle of receiving a lap dance by an enthusiastic college-aged partygoer.

"See that pack of girls? The one wriggling on top of Danny must be with them," Leigh said, keeping herself far enough away from the outdoor bar to remain hidden. Eva was toying with her bracelet, taking in the scene before her.

"How can you tell?"

"They all have that plastic resort bracelet on, plus all the girls look alike. Go buy them a round of shots."

"Where will you be?"

"Lying low, I have the feeling that everyone is looking for me."

"Stay close to me," Eva begged.

"I'll meet you back at Benicio's car," Leigh replied. "Just remember, if anything happens I'll come get you. Where you go, I go," Before completely disappearing she gave one last piece of advice. "Go flirt!"

Eva approached the bar with a stomach full of nerves. But as luck would have it, the entire pack was well inebriated. After a few tequila rounds, and some tactical compliments of the girls' dresses, Eva was readily accepted into the group.

She edged closer to the blonde who was now thrusting her hips into the lap of Danny, who himself looked stone cold sober and adequately lustful. Eva pulled the girl, a junior from the University of Mesa, to her side.

"He does NOT look drunk enough. I think it's time for a body shot!"

"Body shot!" the blonde roared. Surprisingly enough, Danny let himself be pulled to the bar to suck several shots off of young ladies.

"Me next!" cried Eva, her heart thumping. If she was found out, she would be found out now. She prayed Danny would not notice that the girl with the straight, black hair of a few nights ago was now this person standing before him, head full of curls.

She shimmied up on to the bar, adjusting her hot pink dress to particular advantage. Staring at Danny, she rolled her top down to reveal her black lace bra. Lying down, she took the tequila bottle and poured one full shot into her belly button. Danny didn't even make eye contact, but rather placed one hand strategically on her left breast and sucked the tequila down. After that, the rest was easy.

Late into the night, Danny extolled Eva with tales of his shrewd business acumen and luxurious resort home in Merida. Eva acted her part and pretended to be impressed, even whispering how she would like to see his place in Merida.

"We're just here tonight—we are staying in a resort a few miles away."

"La Playa?" he stated, trying to impress her again with his vast local knowledge.

"That's it!" she squealed. She was now certain he did not recognize her, which made her even more intent on her goal. Get him alone, get him to talk, and then kill him.

"Here, call me tomorrow." Danny hastily began scribbling his number on a napkin, when his cell phone began ringing shrilly. Eva snatched it from his fingers with her teeth. Before answering the phone, he grabbed her face and drew a long, lingering kiss, crushing the napkin as he did. Eva tried to hide her grimace as he all but booted her off his lap to answer the phone. Eva retreated back to the party, tucking the number safely away before Danny found her a few minutes later.

"I'll be there tomorrow, with my entire crew. Call me and I'll come pick you up, let's say around 8 pm? Bring your friends, but only girls," he slurred, clumsily pinching her cheek. Eva giggled.

"Only girls," Eva responded, winking at him. He retreated past the group. She gratefully downed glasses of water from the bartender, then looked at her phone—it was nearly 2 am. She easily ducked away from the group and walked out to the parking lot. At first she didn't see anyone in Benicio's car, but then almost jumped a foot when Leigh's head popped out from behind the wheel.

"I didn't think I'd see you again," Leigh said, voice cracking.

"Wow, thanks for sending me then," muttered Eva drunkenly. She shoved the napkin on Leigh's lap, who retrieved it with interest.

"Is this . . . ?"

"Danny's cell phone. He wants us to come over tomorrow, girls only. He'll bring his friends."

"Clever girl," responded Leigh, starting the car and easing it out of the resort and down the highway.

*

"There's still time to practice shooting more," Leigh ventured, pulling into the La Playa resort in the early morning hour.

"Why aren't we going to Benicio's?" Eva sat up, shaking off the vestiges of sleep.

"I have to pee. I sat in that car forever while you got drunk and hit on Danny."

"Because you asked me to."

"Because I asked you to," Leigh responded, smiling.

"Do you want anything?"

"No, let's just get moving."

Eva watched Leigh disappear into the reception area. Only maintenance workers and the cleaning crews were milling around at this hour. After several minutes had passed, Eva began dozing off when a rap came at the window

"You lost, Señorita?"

Startled, she nearly flew out of the seat.

"Whoa, calm down, just checking on you," the man responded, holding his hands up and chuckling. He was tall and lanky, wearing a white outfit many of the other workers wore. She looked at the brass name tag and committed it to memory.

Juan.

Something about how he was looking at her didn't seem quite right. Eva noticed headlights in her rearview mirror.

"Excuse me." She adjusted her skirt and opened the door. He moved back, blocking her path, and she gave out a little cry. "I have to pee, move!"

She gave another cry and he moved to one side. She tried hard not to run and almost knocked over Leigh on her way towards the ladies room. Grabbing Leigh's arm, Eva took several large steps back towards the reception area, past the front desk, and hid behind a large column.

"Someone followed us,"

"What do you mean? How much have you been drinking?"

"No, Leigh. The car, Benicio's car, it must have been that . . . they must have surveillance everywhere, we must have looked suspicious," Eva said. Leigh peered behind the side of the column.

"Well now what? We can't stay here."

"No," Eva agreed, listening for footsteps in the reception area.

"If you really think we're being followed, we can't go back to that car."

"How are we going to get back then?" Eva looked around, eyes wide. Leigh looked to one side.

"I have an idea."

*

The golf cart was harder to maneuver than it looked, though it had been shockingly easy to steal. They snatched it outside a service entrance near the lobby and used the phone's GPS from there. Though it took more than double the time compared to the car, it was blessedly early enough in the morning that they passed undetected to Benicio's house.

The household was still sleeping when they returned. Gia was passed out on the couch, and the silence from the back room suggested that both Benicio and his mother were out cold. They both slumped into the empty couch opposite Gia.

"Do you think you can sleep?"

"Are you kidding, my buzz is wearing off, I'm starving, and I have a headache."

"Let's at least try. Tomorrow is going to be interesting." As they tried to settle themselves into sleep, Eva whispered back at Leigh.

"Do you think they know we're here?"

Leigh pondered this, fighting back the urge to close her eyes and keep them closed.

"It's only a matter of time."

"Can we risk it?"

Leigh massaged her aching temples before offering a response.

"We don't have anywhere else to go."

13

The morning brought some much needed food and coffee to their systems. Benicio had left early, taking the golf cart with him. Leigh didn't ask how Eva explained the cart's presence to Benicio, she just busied herself with devouring whatever food Benicio's mom placed before them.

The day slipped by quickly, as it usually did when the girls had been up for the entirety of the night. It was around 5 pm, just as they started getting ready for their night out with Danny, when the package arrived.

Benicio's mother accepted the brown parcel paper from who Leigh assumed was a local delivery man. She hadn't thought to ask for more details. Midway through applying her makeup, she heard screaming coming from the kitchen. After bolting in, she saw Gia passed out on the floor and Eva standing, pale faced beside Benicio's mother.

For a minute, Leigh thought her friend had done something to Gia, seeing her on the ground with Eva standing above her. It took a few minutes for her to realize that a large cooler in the middle of the kitchen table was pried open, brown paper wrappings strewn beside it.

From her vantage point in the hallway she could only identify what looked like streaks of brown on the side. She took a wary step towards the cooler, her perspective slowly unveiling the grisly contents.

Benicio's hands had been placed on either side of his scalped head, a mass of thick red blood pooled in the bottom. Leigh had to administer a few shakes to Benicio's mother before she could quiet down. When Gia roused herself and began screaming hysterically, Leigh ended up locking Gia and Benicio's mother in the bathroom.

"So," Leigh began, as Eva sat on a living room chair, "they know Benicio helped us."

"I wonder what he told them."

"Probably what you told him."

"That we are drug runners for hire?"

"Yes."

"Oh fuck it Leigh, they must know who we are by now. Benicio probably told them our names, they probably have our passports!"

"Calm down," Leigh soothed. "We have to get our shit together for tonight."

"Tonight? No way. We're not going, this is out of control, we have to . . . "

"To what?" Leigh shouted, trying to be heard above the whimpers coming from the bathroom. "What else can we do Eva?" Eva began sobbing uncontrollably, her brown shoulders shaking.

"Stop," Leigh said in a quieter voice, "you'll ruin your makeup."

The shakes turned into spasms of laughter, as Eva began giggling.

"Oh yes, my makeup. How could I forget. My friend's head and hands are in a cooler, but we have to look good tonight."

Leigh smiled, and then cast a wary eye at the cooler.

"Go get ready. I have to do something."

Leaving Eva to fix her makeup in the bedroom, Leigh went to the kitchen and grabbed the tequila bottle, taking a long drink before preparing for her grisly task. After grabbing some gloves left on the counter, Leigh dragged the cooler to the compound where the weapons cache was located.

"Alright," she said to herself out loud, straightening. She first pulled Benicio's right hand from the cooler, shuddering at how rubbery it felt. Gently, she scanned the fingerprint. The machine echoed back a beep. The next part she was really dreading. Taking a deep breath, she lifted up the head, or what remained of it, and pulled the eyelid on the right eye open wide, just in front of the retinal scanner.

The machine chirped back and the door clicked open. Fighting back nausea, she placed the head back in the cooler and quickly let herself in. Before venturing back into the darkness, Leigh paused.

She thought about Benicio, how well-meaning he had been. She shouldn't have used him so carelessly. But she was determined to get the better of Guero, by whatever means. Did that make her heartless? What about Eva, was it fair to keep pulling her further down the rabbit hole?

A flash of metal caught her eye from the depths of the cooler. Looking closer, Leigh fished out a pair of Benicio's sunglasses that had been tossed in beside him. Breathing slowly, she carefully wiped off the blood-stained glasses. Slowly, putting every rational thought in her mind away, she put them on.

Feeling calm creep alongside her, she placed her hands in her pockets and began walking down the brick-lined corridor, mentally preparing herself for the night ahead. The lights illuminated the dark metal of Guero's weapons stockpile at the end of the hallway. Leigh carefully began loading up Gia's discarded duffle bags with semi-automatic weapons.

She had the second bag nearly full when she spied a machete, leaning next to the brick wall in a tangle of discarded rope. Straightening, Leigh walked over to it and picked it up, gently touching the edge of the weapon with her finger. It was slightly rusted, but seemingly no worse for wear. The weapon answered back, and she studied the line of red that had formed where she had placed her finger.

"Bad ass!" Leigh said aloud, swooshing the weapon in the air with enthusiasm. Reaching behind her, she found it neatly fit in the elastic of her bra. Pleased, she finished loading up the rest of the clips for the weapons, and zipped the duffle bags shut.

Eva was setting her face in powder when Leigh returned, calling out to her from the kitchen.

"Call Danny, have him come get us."

"Here?"

"No, the resort. The more he thinks we are staying there, the safer we are here."

"What about . . . Benicio?"

"Let's not worry about that just now," Leigh said, walking into the living room, heels in hand.

"Leigh?"

"Yes." Leigh turned to face her friend—Eva was decked out in another one of Gia's short black dresses.

"Are you ready?"

Leigh didn't answer, but handed Eva the phone.

"Call."

They were able to hitch a ride to the resort from a pack of maintenance workers. After several minutes fending off wandering hands, they entered the gates of the La Playa without incident.

"Where are we meeting him?" Leigh asked, adjusting the heavy bundles of semiautomatic rifles and ammunition. They had been graciously off loaded at the reception area, and she was rearranging the bags at her feet as they waited.

"Here. At the reception area," Eva responded, looking at the bags. "How are we going to explain the duffle bags?"

"We'll just say we brought stuff for a sleepover."

"Oh, sounds good," Eva responded. They stood quietly, eyeing each car pull up, thinking it was their ride, only to watch it pull away. "Want to tell me what the plan is?" Eva offered softly, twirling a shiny curl in one hand, keeping her eyes on the flow of incoming cars.

"We need to find where they moved the drugs," Leigh said, fingering the machete. It was safety positioned against her upper back, secured by her bra strap.

"And if we don't find out?"

"We have to. If we don't, we'll make a run for it."

"And if they get us first?"

"We'll make it," responded Leigh with determination, pulling her eyes away from the reception area to look at her friend. "Ever wish," she began haltingly, "you can make one of your lies come true?"

Eva gave her a confused look, so Leigh continued.

"I used to tell everyone I was an only child, so no one would ask where my sister was. After a while, I used to start wishing that lie was true. Life would have been so much easier."

"Are you lying to me when you say we are going to make it Leigh?" Eva asked, still unsure what they were talking about.

"I'm telling you I'm going to will it into happening," Leigh said, wiping off the beads of sweat that formed on her brow.

Eva didn't reply, taking up the challenge once again of scanning the horizon for their ride. A few moments later, a dark, armored car pulled up to the curb.

"This has to be him," Eva said under her breath. Leigh averted her face and busied herself with the bags while Danny showered kisses on Eva's cheeks. As he turned to introduce himself, Leigh felt her chest tighten.

"Pleased to meet you," he said. Danny masked his surprise very well, but it was obvious he recognized her. Taking Leigh's hand, he placed it to his lips. Leigh giggled and pulled her hand away quickly, pretending to be coy. It was a useful distraction, and as he straightened he said something in Spanish.

"What?" Leigh smirked, looking at Eva who smiled.

"Nothing," Danny replied, smiling at her with a wolf-like grin. He paused. "I was just thinking about how fortunate today has been."

He opened the door, and Leigh settled herself behind the driver's seat, her duffle bag placed firmly beside her. Eva chattered away in the passenger seat, trying her best to hide her nervousness. Leigh didn't know if Eva captured the full intent of her strategic seating arrangement, but she most certainly was on to the fact that Danny now knew who they were. Hopefully, Leigh thought, he had no idea they had set him up.

14

As the houses whizzed past, Danny couldn't help but congratulate himself. He had captured the girls who couldn't be caught, and it was all thanks to fate! He was a well-respected foot solider, and a favorite of Guero's. He would surely be promoted as a result.

Danny thought of different ways he could retell the story, navigating the car away from the resort. He didn't live far, and had only driven a short while before he began pulling up the private drive to his home.

Trying to contain his excitement at the wicked plan now forming in his mind, he called off security awaiting his entrance with a few clicks on his phone. He would have his fun with the two of them first, he decided, and would then bring them inside for his men.

He had bought the place because of its strategic remoteness and the balcony overlooking a stunning view of the ocean. This was very handy for tossing enemies over, where they met their end on the cliffs below. Danny smiled to himself, preparing for his night of debauchery. After he was done with them, the girls would join his other victims, falling conveniently off the balcony, their spring break over for good.

He had made sure his men were ready for the forthcoming entertainment. They had been supplied with plenty of booze earlier in the day, and were ready for the main event. Nearly his entire crew had come, which made him proud. He would take them with him when he accepted the new position. Danny was running all these scenarios through his head in a matter of minutes, his face beaming.

He was almost to the front of the drive when he felt the wind leave him, followed by a tightening grasp around his neck. He felt a flood of warmth, and wondered if his nose was bleeding. His initial reaction was embarrassment, but then he realized that there was blood everywhere, on the steering wheel, his new suit.

He saw the flash of the machete bury itself into his throat, and he knew distinctly that placing Leigh behind him had been a mistake. He went to yell, but a bubbling gurgle was all that emitted from his mangled throat. He looked aghast at Eva, who calmly picked up a plastic bag from the middle console, placed it over his head, and squeezed.

15

"Fuck," cried Leigh. "I have blood on my top."

"It's black, you can hardly see it," Eva responded, making sure Danny had stopped moving.

"True," responded Leigh, breathing a bit heavily, but no worse for wear after killing Danny. They removed his cigarettes, and Eva took it upon herself to light up.

"Thanks for telling me when you were going to do it." Eva shot Leigh a dirty look, passing the cigarette to her friend.

"Would have ruined the surprise," Leigh began, taking a long drag. She then softened her criticism. "You would have been anxious, and I didn't want to give anything away." Eva frowned, but then nodded in agreement.

"Damn you Leigh, why are you good at this?"

"I have no idea," Leigh said as she exhaled. "I see it in my head before I do it. Besides, we really don't have a choice at this point." She stopped herself, unzipping the duffle bag and handing a semi-automatic to Eva. Leigh grabbed some extra magazines and stuck them into the elastic of her underwear.

Dresses hiked up to allow for quick reloading, they exited the car and began to slowly walk up the stairs to the house.

"My guess is his little party is in the back of the house," Leigh said, as they advanced toward the ornate front entrance.

"Agreed. How do we surprise them? What's the layout?" Leigh stood at the door and frowned.

"I don't know. What if you went in first?"

"Ok, I'm getting really tired of always having to go in first . . ."

"Eva, I'm just wondering if . . . "

"No, I'm sick of this, you go in first." They were practically shouting at each other now, and Leigh belatedly realized there was probably all kinds of surveillance on the compound. She turned to her friend.

"Fuck it, let's just go in there and shoot!" Leigh shouted back in frustration.

"Fine," Eva snapped, temper getting the best of her.

Opening the door together, they took several brisk steps into the threshold. Sounds from the back of the house directed their path to the group outside. It took no more than five seconds for them to clear the foyer, which opened into an impressive living space. Balcony doors were open, which overlooked high cliffs and the ocean below.

Leigh was the first to shoot, closely followed by Eva. Either the men didn't have their guns or were simply too inebriated to get to them in time. Moving right to left, Eva and Leigh advanced on their targets like fish in a barrel. The pair worked in perfect tandem, reminiscent of their practice at Benicio's gun range. When Leigh paused to reload, Eva disposed of a man who was pulling out his cell phone. After their work was done, in addition to a quick round to make sure no one was moving, they stood in silence.

"Bathroom," whispered Eva, nodding her head in the direction of a closed door situated near the room they had just destroyed. They positioned themselves on either side.

As the door flung open, a man shuffled forward, his pants wrapped around his ankles. He threw his hands up and Leigh promptly shot him in the leg. He went down with a yelp.

"Eva, grab his leg," commanded Leigh. Without a word, Eva picked up his uninjured leg while Leigh grabbed the other. Leigh nodded her head toward the balcony doors. Together they dragged him past the dead bodies of his companions out onto the tiled surface.

Once outside, they dragged him to the edge of the generously sized balcony. Danny didn't think much of safety. A sparse railing was the only object that separated the edge of the balcony with the cliffs below. They positioned his body easily under the railing, perpendicular to the edge, head hovering over the open air. Dropping his leg, Leigh retrieved the machete from her makeshift holster.

Eva moved behind her, and took a place near the railing to make sure their hostage wasn't moving. Leigh eased one leg over the railing, fighting off a twinge of fear at seeing the coastline so far below. Her lean legs now straddling the railing, she held the machete at his throat.

"Ask him where the drugs are," she said to Eva.

"My Spanish sucks."

"Use your shitty Spanish then. Ask him!" Leigh demanded, adrenaline coursing through her veins. In stumbling Spanish, Eva shouted a few inquiries. Each one was met by a shake of the head.

Leigh slowly began speaking. "I would start talking before I cut you up into little itty bitty pieces," she growled. The man's eyes rolled back into his head as Leigh readied her machete.

"Ask again," Leigh commanded, this time sure she would get a satisfactory response.

Eva repeated her request to a now stuttering hostage. As he began babbling, Eva nodded.

"Well, I can tell you what he said but it doesn't make much sense."

"Last chance," Leigh responded, holding the machete firmly with both hands and resting it on his neck.

"Wait," the man said in English, surprising them both.

"I'm listening," Leigh responded, keeping her hands steady. He took a breath and continued.

"The Cenotillo cenote. We stashed it in the rock ledge. I can show you . . . for a price."

"No," Leigh replied, steadying her hand. "I'm tired of negotiating. And I know where it is."

With this response, the man's eyes darkened. He spat at Leigh and smirked. "You're dead, *brujas*."

"You first." Leigh raised the machete high then fluidly sliced the blade through her target's neck. His head tumbled downward towards the ocean, a thin red ribbon trailing behind.

Leigh looked at Eva, who nodded back with grim determination.

"We should probably line them up on the railing and cut all their heads off. For Benicio."

"While Benicio was a great guy," Leigh replied, wiping the blade with the cloth from her dress, "I don't think I can handle that right now. Let's find some car keys and get out of here."

Returning to Danny's car to remove their duffle bags, they surveyed their choice of vehicles.

"All of these cars look pretty obvious to me. We might as well write 'cartel' on each of them. Isn't there something more discreet?" Eva asked, frowning.

"I know, let's pick the one that looks the least cartel-like." Leigh was walking from one car to the next, eyeing the interiors.

"They are all black armored cars," Eva responded, still unconvinced.

"Ok then, just pick a key, we'll go with whichever one it opens."

After returning to the carnage of Danny's living room, they gathered several keys from the unmoving bodies.

"This one," Leigh proclaimed, drawing a key at random. Clicking the electronic key, the car closest to Eva came to life.

Discarding the other keys hastily, they loaded the car with their bags of ammunition.

After this was completed, Leigh eased herself behind the wheel as Eva busied herself with her phone, directing the GPS navigation with a few clicks of her fingers.

"Thank you, GPS. Can you imagine how much harder this would have been without it?"

"Do you have Facebook on that?" Leigh asked, carefully guiding the car down Danny's private driveway while Eva fiddled with her cell phone. "I want to update my status."

"You just executed someone, and now you want to check your status?"

"We do have parents you know. Or more importantly, Joy and Gia do," Leigh answered. "We're going to have to come up with a more plausible story to their parents than the one we told Benicio."

"I can post a status update for all of us," Eva began, thinking along the same lines.

"Say we're drinking on the beach or something."

"I'm one step ahead of you," Eva responded, typing enthusiastically.

"We should use Joy and Gia's phones as well!" Leigh snapped her fingers. "They must have been calling, right?" Eva scanned the phones in her lap.

"We have too many fucking cell phones, Leigh."

"I know, let's just . . ." she looked at the devices in her friend's lap. "Well, obviously Gia's is that pink one."

Eva scanned the call history.

"Only one missed call from Gia's dad, what should I do?"

"Listen to the voicemail."

Eva sat for a few minutes checking, while Leigh dutifully followed the navigation.

"Just checking in . . ." Eva began as she repeated back the message from Gia's dad.

"Text him back, say we are enjoying the resort."

"Gia would never thank her father."

"True, don't respond."

"What about Joy's phone?"

Leigh was silent for a few minutes. "Update the status on Facebook, but that's it."

After posting a fake status, Eva put the phones back in her purse. They were almost to Benicio's house when Eva brought up a new subject.

"What's next?"

"We need to get to the cenote and pick up the drugs. We use them as ransom so Guero lets us go."

Eva pondered this in silence.

"We can't recover it ourselves," Leigh added. Now at Benicio's, she turned off the engine. Looking up, she spotted graffiti strategically placed next to one of the low structures Benicio had been guarding for Los Muertos.

"What does that say?" Leigh asked, nodding toward the graffiti. It looked fresh and certainly was not there a few hours before.

"Looks like it says La Familia," Eva responded. She paused before continuing, looking at Leigh with a little smile. "Are you thinking what I'm thinking?

16

Guero swirled the last of the beer and took a satisfying gulp. It had been a long day. He had not yet heard from Danny, but he assumed no news was good news. He also assumed his product had been dealt with. The American girls, he was still figuring out. As for himself, cleaning up after Jiménez had been a pesky task. He had personally gone to the Cancun resort to make sure the room had been cleaned properly, that no blood had been left on any surface, and no traces of violence remained.

He had then collected the passports of the four women who had been registered under that room and erased their information from the system. After that, it would be hard to prove that any of it ever happened. For all intents and purposes, the girls never arrived in Mexico. The women in the passport photos all looked very young. If they were fakes—and these girls were in the pay of La Familia—they were very good ones. He paused on each image, trying to determine who might be the person he had spoken to on the phone. The one who had been hired to start a war.

There must be some connection to La Familia. There had to be. They were angling for territory in Cancun, and the turf war was starting to bubble over. Though they had many recruits, La Familia didn't understand the complexities of the business, and their sloppy handiwork drew unwanted attention.

Guero relied on the tourist dollar and the resorts, it was necessary to make the money clean, legitimate. And tourists didn't mix very well with violent shoot outs and heads in coolers. He wanted to make his illicit activities as clean and business-like as possible. What was the point of making things bloody and messy? Only as a last resort. Then make it as bloody and messy as possible. To make sure they never forget.

Yes, things had gotten more complicated. He remembered the good old days. Though he never had much growing up in Laredo, he loved his aunt and uncle dearly. The warm, generous couple was such a contrast to his cold and irrational mother.

"It's the drugs," they would tell him, but deep down he knew it was really him. He drove her to the drugs. Not the reverse.

"Guero," she used to call him, mockingly. His father was a gringo and Guero's light eyes and fair hair seemed to insult her. It only seemed fitting to retain the name once he ascended in the ranks in the cartel. The women loved him, the men feared him. Business had been good. This changed when La Familia entered the scene.

Danny wasn't answering his cell phone, so Guero decided to go find Danny for himself. He was probably down at his pool with some girl. Danny liked picking them up at the resorts and taking them to his private residence after slipping something in their drink.

In this respect, Guero could understand Jiménez's style of slow seduction. At least he bought them dinner. Guero had spoken to Danny numerous times, but figured he wasn't getting through to him. Some men just hated women.

As Guero pulled up to the drive, he was struck by the number of cars in the driveway. Were they meeting to discuss business? Was this a potential coup? Nearly every one of his men were accounted for when he looked at the plates and counted the cars before going in. As he slowly climbed the staircase, his mood soured more on the recent turn of events.

Blindsided by some rogue agent in a rival cartel, and then forced to eliminate Jiménez and his men after months of them skimming from the top. Now he had to find a new resort manager. And now this! An unauthorized meeting. What were they up to?

He had worked himself up so much that when he entered the residence he practically tripped over the first body. As he caught himself, he looked down in disbelief, and then toward the carnage.

The stillness of the scene put him on edge. Slowly, he reached for his gun and held it at his side. There was no need—this was nearly everyone. Sensing movement on the patio, he opened the door cautiously. Jose, or what was left of him, was being fed on by birds, his headless form trapped beneath the balcony railing.

Stepping back inside, Guero moved quickly through the house and down the stairs. It was then he noticed Danny's car, and a pile of discarded car keys lying on the ground. Gun still in hand, he moved towards the passenger seat.

As he got closer to the tinted window, he saw Danny's body slumped over the steering wheel. Opening the door, he removed the plastic bag and was struck by the handiwork. This was a killing filled with rage, intensely personal.

Hands steady, Guero placed his gun back into his holster before completing a cursory search of the car. On the floor, behind Danny, was a discarded cigarette. The butt was covered in pink lip gloss.

17

They goaded Benicio's mother out of the bathroom and fended off dagger-like stares from Gia, who made a beeline for the bedroom. Eva explained in stumbling Spanish that they went to avenge Benicio's killers, showing her the blood on their arms and clothes. His mother rolled her eyes heavenward and began another round of wailing, thanking her "angels" for avenging her son's death.

"Tell her these angels are hungry," Leigh responded, walking to the bathroom to shower. After she emerged they shared a silent meal. When she was finished, Leigh pushed her plate aside, a plan forming in her mind.

"Both Jiménez and Benicio mentioned rivals. La Familia in particular," she began, pointing out the window to the graffiti they spotted earlier. "That looks like evidence that they are in this area. They are tagging all around here, and you said yourself that Benicio told you they were moving in on Los Muertos' territory."

"Who cares?" Gia muttered, off in her own land, pushing food around her plate. Both girls ignored her as Leigh continued.

"Let's say we helped their little turf war along by offering up Los Muertos' hidden drugs?" Leigh responded. Eva nodded in agreement.

"If we convinced La Familia we were nothing but a bunch of dumb recruits, we would have the help we need to get the drugs out of the cenote."

"We'll need an introduction though."

Leigh looked at Benicio's mother, who was flipping her rosary.

"Señora," Leigh said, "does this place have a bar?"

*

"You so outta place here!" the bartender yelled at them over the music. "Most tourists don't come out this far." His English was very bad, but he was good natured and generous with the drinks.

They were seated at a local drinking hole which was tagged generously on the outside with La Familia's signature graffiti. It was dark inside, and they had immediately taken places at the bar hoping to draw some kind of attention. It didn't take long.

"We're staying with a friend who lives here," Leigh yelled back, wrapping her fingers around the Tecate and taking a long drink. She smiled at Eva and motioned her eyes to the back of the bar. Eva didn't have to turn, she felt the flutter of attention as soon as they had walked through the door. Leigh confirmed this to her casually.

"See, they've already spotted you."

"How do you know they are with the cartels?" Eva shot back, focusing on her own beer intently.

"I get the feeling," Leigh responded, pulling some chips near her, "that men with shiny Rolexes aren't out there picking avocados."

Eva nodded, adjusted her outfit, and then turned and smiled at the group. The men smiled back and one beckoned the girls over. Leigh led the way.

"How do we tell which cartel?" Eva asked through a clenched smile.

"I have no idea," replied Leigh. The two approached and made hasty introductions.

Eva only caught one name, Manuel. While Leigh focused her attention on a youngish, moustached patron, Eva attempted to make small talk with Manuel in bad Spanish. It took some effort— he had an unsightly cleft, which glistened at Eva from the seedy glow of the overhead lighting. It was near 2 am when she hit pay dirt.

"My friend and I are soooo broke," she began, slurring her

words. "We can't leave until we make some money, so we can buy a plane ticket back."

"Oh no!" he cried, moving himself to best advantage beneath her lap. Eva gestured dramatically.

"No, you misunderstand. We need big money. Maybe we take something back in our luggage, stuff like that. You know how to do that?"

He played coy a bit, but his ego eventually won out.

"I might. I might know. You came into the right bar, that's for sure. I'm in charge of new recruits for what we call La Familia." Eva had her doubts, but still, it was the connection they had been looking for. As he continued, she became more convinced he knew what he was talking about.

"We don't do it here—we go further in the jungle. That's where we train you. We have all kinds there. Americans, English, the Europeans. You come out, pick up your stash, learn a few tricks, and we send you across."

"I'd want it worth my while though, I want a big payout," Eva pouted, taking a drink of her beer and watching his eyes on her.

"You take as much as you want!" Manuel exclaimed. "I can take you there, you'll see."

"My friend too?"

"Man, I won't take you without her," Manuel replied, rolling his eyes at an inebriated Leigh, who was now attempting to give her companion a lap dance. Eva pulled her off, and excused themselves.

"Tomorrow morning," she told Leigh, who had drunkenly inquired as to their progress. It was unlike Leigh to let loose and let Eva take the lead. For some reason, it made Eva proud.

As they began trudging back to Benicio's house, Eva filled Leigh in on the details. "He is coming to the bar to meet us and will take us to the camp, in the jungle."

"I don't have clothes for that," Leigh cried in mock alarm, kicking off her heels before picking them up and walking down the dirt path behind Eva, who followed suit, giggling. Walking into Benicio's house, taking up residence on the beat-up couches, they congratulated themselves on their good fortune. Things were going according to plan.

18

The sky was lightening when Leigh rose, showered, and dressed for the day. She put on a comfortable beach outfit, tucking a long dress shirt around her miniskirt, careful to hide her machete in its makeshift holster, and belting the ensemble. While she had chosen the most loose and practical garment, they hadn't exactly packed for a day trip to the jungle. Leigh was also careful to pack her favored handgun in her purse, hoping they wouldn't be searched.

They decided against leaving Gia, after clear indications from Benicio's mother that she was no longer welcome in her house.

"She said she was doing drugs in the bathroom," Eva translated, finishing off her breakfast and quickly dumping some provisions in her roomy bag. Leigh went to find Gia, who was awake and semi-coherent.

"Take your bag, you're coming with us."

Leigh paused to study her. Despite the conditions, and the fact Gia hadn't been eating, she was still beautiful. Her blonde curls had gone frizzy and wild in the heat, which only further heightened the pigment of her clear blue eyes. She looked like some jungle creature, wild and unpredictable.

"Shower, please," Leigh said, "and get dressed."

They made the trek back to the bar in silence. If Gia wondered where they were going, she neglected to ask. It was just after sunrise when Manuel met them. He greeted Eva with a smile, the cleft gleaming. After a flourish of introductions, he crawled behind the wheel of a red Jeep, motioning Eva to take the seat beside him. Gia and Leigh took their places in the back of the Jeep.

It was slow going, and there were no seat belts. Each passenger had to hold on to avoid tumbling out into the jungle. The vegetation was thick and green, the humidity drenching the group in sweat.

After a few hours, they stopped to rest. Leigh was grateful for the pit stop, and she eased her aching limbs out to the side in a glorious stretch. Nodding at her from the front seat, Eva exited the Jeep, departing into the thick foliage to relieve herself. She was shortly followed by Manuel, who wiped off sweat from his brow with his arm as he disappeared into the jungle.

After both had left the vehicle, Leigh carefully pulled out the gun from her purse, sliding it under the floor mat of the Jeep. Gia shifted next to her, and Leigh realized she was not, as she previously had assumed, asleep. Slowly, Gia climbed out of the Jeep, wandering into the foliage where Leigh assumed she would partake of her stash.

Now alone in the car, Leigh took her machete from its holster, and slipped it snugly between the seat cushions. Just in case, Leigh thought to herself. After what seemed like too brief of a stop, Manuel gave a shout. Leigh only had time to take care of her own necessary business before climbing back into the Jeep to continue their journey. Leigh's stomach told her it was around lunchtime when they arrived.

Her instincts from earlier were right—they were searched as soon as they exited the Jeep. It wasn't an aggressive search, just a friendly one of necessity, with smiles all round from the men who had greeted them. After this was completed to Manuel's satisfaction, Leigh allowed herself a quick survey of their destination.

It looked like a guerilla camp straight out of some bad action movie, consisting of huts and curling smoke coming from several structures situated in a semicircle. Manuel gave a short, boastful tour, from the meth lab (Leigh assumed that was the reason for all the glass tubing), to packets of miscellaneous materials she assumed was either heroin or cocaine.

Even though her hunger was starting to get the best of her, and Gia was beginning to twitch, Leigh felt frozen on the tour, unable to muster more than a smile at the many piles and packets of clean, white powder.

"Now, the boss wants to meet you!" Manuel stammered in English, after concluding their little tour. Leigh looked at Eva, clad in a bright blue dress, looking more like a beach goer than someone on a jaunt at the local cartel hideaway. Eva turned, leading the way, with Leigh following suit and Gia trailing slowly behind.

Their destination was a sturdy building of taupe stucco, which would have looked right at home in any Phoenix suburb. When they entered, Leigh felt like she had walked into one. Flat screens donned the walls, a pool table took up much of the back room, and every possible accommodation had been thought of. A wiry young man, probably no more than 30, rose from a sofa chair to greet them.

"Well, now where are you from? NO wait! Let me guess, California?" Before they could answer he motioned to Manuel. "Keys, my man." On cue, Manuel tossed the Jeep's keys to him with a smile.

"Phoenix, actually," Eva responded, looking at Leigh to try and figure out which one of them was going to have the best rapport with their new acquaintance.

"Arizona Southern University," said Leigh, who held his brown eyes for a few seconds before they settled on Gia. Leigh glanced at Eva, whose expression was the smallest of "ah-ha's."

"And who is this?" he asked, gesturing towards Gia, still looking like a deer-in-the-headlights in her barely-there beach cover up and platform sandals.

"This is Gia, and you are?" Leigh inquired, still taking stock of their surroundings.

"Call me the Matador!" he cried, spreading his hands out to his sides for emphasis. His face broke into a wide grin, which made his wiry goatee look that more pathetic.

"You're from Texas?" Eva inquired.

"Nah, Long Beach."

Leigh raised her eyebrows in surprise. The Matador threw his head back and laughed.

"Plain as print that face of yours, I know exactly what you're thinking."

"What am I thinking then?" inquired Leigh, sizing him up.

"What is some hippie from Long Beach doing in the middle of the jungle working for a drug cartel?" The Matador smiled.

"La Familia?" inquired Eva.

"Who else? They own Cancun," Matador responded cockily. He whipped his head around. "You must be hungry—and thirsty, beer time." He gestured towards Gia, who let out the slightest of giggles, and she followed his lead into a generously stocked kitchen.

"Maria will make you anything you like."

"Tacos for me, please, we're famished," offered Leigh, as a small, middle-aged woman smiled and began preparing something that soon smelled wonderful. The Matador was not one to let silence rule the day. He regaled them with tales of his prowess in the Long Beach drug market, how he owned four houses in California and one in Cancun.

"And one here?" Leigh responded. The Matador didn't miss a beat.

"Well, not really, the cartel owns this one. Which I guess means I do, because I am the fucking cartel! Ha ha!" He shoved a taco in his mouth, and while munching, stared at Gia, who was only picking at her food, but had forced down half a taco. Her eyeliner was drooping a bit in the heat, but this seemed to enhance, rather than diminish, the Matador's admiration.

After lunch, Manuel departed, and they retired to a back patio for beers. Leigh felt the warm buzz of alcohol as she propped herself on the arm of a wicker chaise. The Matador brought up the reason for their visit.

"So, the boys tell me you're looking to make some money?"

"A lot," admitted Eva, exchanging glances with Leigh.

"You might make more selling yourselves than running drugs," the Matador laughed, shooting another glance at Gia.

"What do you mean?" Leigh asked, peeling the label of her beer. She knew exactly what he meant, but felt like having it explained to her.

"My cartel," he stopped to take a swig of beer, "we also run women. Pretty ones. People pay. The cuter, the better. You make a million easy that way."

"For a human life?" asked Eva.

"For a slave," the Matador responded, pulling at his goatee and shrugging. He had obviously enjoyed his time in the jungle. Gifted with average looks, his confident personality easily made up for his scrawny features. He had certainly been eating well, if the paunch in his stomach was any indication.

"We're not that desperate, not yet," Leigh sniffed in response.

"Why do you want the money so badly then?" he asked, with genuine curiosity rather than suspicion. He was on his seventh beer, and Leigh got the feeling he enjoyed the company of his American compatriots more than he let on.

"Tuition . . . shopping," Leigh replied, which was answered by another round of laughter from the Matador.

"Fine, I'll give you some shit to run. But you buy the stuff from me first, that way you take extra care of it."

"Don't need to, we already have some," Leigh replied, downing her beer and reaching for another. It took the Matador a few seconds, but he caught on.

"Have some of what?" He asked, eyes sparkling. Leigh shrugged at the question.

"I'm telling you I have some product. I don't know what it is and I don't want to know."

"How much do you have of this mystery product?" The Matador asked, sinewy hands gripping the beer in anticipation.

"Lots," responded Leigh, smiling and taking a drink. "But you have to help us get it first, we don't have the manpower. And you have to guarantee we get paid, after we drop it off."

"I can do that, shit, I am . . . "

"The cartel," Leigh finished for him. The Matador smiled.

"How do I know you're legit?"

Leigh nodded at Gia.

"Show him Gia."

Blinking, Gia fished her private stash from her bag, offering it to the Matador like a peace offering.

He studied its wrappings with interest, seemingly recognizing a distinct pattern. Looking up, he smiled.

"You got it, baby!"

Finishing her beer, Leigh removed her shirt to reveal her bikini top. She threw the shirt on the ground.

"Feel like dancing, Eva?"

Eva jumped a bit, obviously thinking about something else.

"Sure."

The Matador smiled rakishly at Leigh. "Shit, I should have known when you walked in you'd be trouble."

"No trouble, just looking for a good time." Leigh stood and began circling her hips to an imaginary beat.

A few beers and an iPod playlist later, everyone, including Gia, had loosened up. The Matador wouldn't let any of his men in, though his phone kept ringing intermittently. Leigh didn't get the sense that many young women came to this camp very often.

She was dancing around with Eva when Eva's eyes widened. Turning, she saw the Matador had finally made his move. He had Gia on the pool table, who was giggling uproariously.

"He looks like a sloppy kisser," Eva said, rolling her eyes and doing a twirl to the beat.

"He's really getting in there," Leigh replied, taking out her phone and beginning to film.

"Leigh!"

"What? Just repaying the favor," Leigh retorted, to Eva's wide smile. She set the phone on the island near the table and snuck out of the room. They escaped just in time to hear very clear indications of the Matador's feelings for Gia.

"Pretty wicked, Leigh." Eva, shaking with laughter, grabbed a beer and sank into a chair. Leigh pulled her hair to one side, and adjusted her bikini top.

"Jesus, I'm getting hungry again."

"Me too."

They sat in silence on the porch, listening to the now more strenuous sounds coming from the house.

"I can't believe I killed Joy," Leigh said suddenly, holding her beer up to the sky then taking a long drink. Eva didn't respond but fumbled with the bottle's label. Leigh looked at her for a few seconds, thinking.

"You knew?"

"I knew," Eva said, peeling the label off and setting it neatly on the table.

"It felt like the right thing to do," Leigh responded with a shrug, chuckling at how insane that sounded. Eva offered her one of Gia's cigarettes, which Leigh took with a nod.

"She was always Gia's right hand," Eva continued, lighting one for herself and taking a drag. "I remember right after I met you guys, Joy told me to join your sorority. So I did, like a good follower." Leigh watched Eva tell it, her body still. At length, she continued.

"And during pledge week, Joy had me lick the sweat off of a bunch of guy's backs. It was disgusting, but you should have seen her face. She loved it, every minute."

"As opposed to Gia, who would have made you do much worse," Leigh offered, taking a long drag.

"No, Gia used to like me. Her Mexican friend, you know? I got the feeling when we talked, she liked the fact that I was different."

"Yeah, I could see that."

"You seemed to have some sort of alliance with her," Eva responded, not intending to come off as jealous. Leigh was silent for a few minutes.

"I let her get away with a lot, because knowing her was always more fun than not knowing her." She paused before continuing. "Gia always left me alone, we understood each other."

"It's cause she knew," Eva replied succinctly, flicking her ash in her dead beer bottle. "She could feel what you were capable of. Joy didn't, which is why she's dead."

Leigh didn't respond, she let the cigarette burn nearly to her fingertips before flicking it in to the bottle.

"Think we can find that cook from earlier?" Leigh turned up an eyebrow hopefully.

"You kidding? She's in bed by now."

"Are they done?"

"Probably." They snuck into the living room to see the bedroom door closed.

"You better delete that video." Eva motioned to Leigh's phone, still recording on the kitchen island. "I'm officially paranoid of leaving any trace of this little adventure behind."

"Awww, but I might want to remember this." Leigh responded, watching a few seconds before deleting it.

"Ok, now I'm really starving," Eva spoke into the empty room, eyeing up the kitchen.

"Let's see what we can dig up," Leigh offered. They took a cursory search of the kitchen, rummaging through the fridge to find leftovers. After a few moments they were rewarded. Over a decent dinner of tacos, they settled themselves on the couch for some much needed sleep.

*

It wasn't long before Leigh felt someone shaking her arm. It was Gia.

"Let's go, we're leaving now."

"What? Why?" Leigh responded, forgetting for a second where she was, and what they had been doing. The second she remembered, she pulled her arm from Gia and looked over to a now stirring Eva.

"We are going to pick up the stash tonight," Gia said, seemingly stone-cold sober.

Roused by the commotion, Leigh lifted herself erect and shook off the few hours of sleep they had. She assumed the Matador must have been up, as the lights were on and there were sounds of movement coming from the bedroom.

"And we are going tonight because . . . ?" Eva said after Gia left the room.

"My thoughts exactly," mumbled Leigh.

Still slightly drunk, the girls hastily gathered their things and followed the Matador to the Jeep in the pitch black.

"It's stashed in the Cenotillo cenote," Leigh said unprompted, once they were on the road, "do you know where it is?"

"You kidding? I toured it when I first came here!" the Matador shot back. In the darkness Leigh could feel Eva's eyes on her, begging for a plan. Still trying to shake off the booze and lack of sleep, Leigh realized the Matador must have known where they were going. They weren't exactly hiding their conversations from Gia, but Leigh assumed she was too drugged up to listen. Or was she?

It took several hours for them to reach the cenote, for which Leigh was grateful. She tried to run through the alphabet back and forth, recite her numbers in Spanish. And above all, avoid Eva's imploring gaze. Sober, sober, sober, she kept telling herself.

As the car shuddered to a halt, Leigh carefully checked the floor mats of the Jeep to retrieve her weapon. Her heart began beating faster as her hands fell on crumbs and discarded gum wrappers. As soberness dawned, she realized with a sinking feeling that the situation had gone from bad to worse. The gun was gone.

19

Guero had been putting off calling Rueben, his boss, for long enough. He made an arrangement to meet with him that night, and then put on his favorite suit, not cutting corners where his outfit was concerned. Rueben kept Guero close, relying on him not only for the business aspect of the resorts, but on the cartel takings as a whole. He trusted Guero, and valued him for what he was—a very crooked businessman who did what he had to in order to squeeze out rivals and revenue.

They met at Rueben's favorite restaurant, La Floresta. The locals knew them and left them distinctly alone. After arriving, Guero waved a greeting to the owners and took a seat opposite Rueben. A few cursory greetings later, they commenced with the small talk. Rueben seemed to be in an odd mood. He grumbled about his wife a bit before he started giving hints to Guero to get to the point.

"By the way," Guero began casually, "I took care of that thieving Jiménez, and all of his men." Rueben stopped eating for a minute, and then continued chewing again with a nod of approval. It was the next part Guero was concerned about. "But what you haven't heard is that shortly after that took place, Danny was massacred, along with *all* of his men."

Rueben froze. Guero knew this bombshell would be the hardest. Danny was one of Rueben's relatives. Despite the fact it was not a close relation, Guero knew this would be perceived differently than the other deaths.

"I have a few appointments today to figure out who is responsible," Guero continued. Rueben did not respond. Guero knew he was waiting to hear that appropriate action had been taken and was willing to wait to speak until Guero could confirm as much.

"I think we both know . . ." Guero began trailing off, "who the responsible party may be."

"La Familia," Rueben stated matter-of-factly. "Finally, they insult me in this way."

"One of them was decapitated," Guero responded, taking a swig from his beer and slamming it down on the table.

"This wouldn't have been possible without an insider," Rueben said, glancing up at him. Guero nodded.

"Benicio, he was in charge of protecting the weapons cache. I took care of him already. There is another traitor, but I'm not ready to eliminate him yet. He still may prove useful," Guero responded.

"Who? No, don't tell me. I trust you," Rueben replied back.

"They also stole some product," Guero lied. Even though he had Danny move the product, he wanted to put the nail firmly in the coffin of La Familia. This statement made Rueben stiffen noticeably. Killing distant relatives was all well and good, but now they were fucking with his money.

"How much?" Rueben asked, wiping off his hands.

"A noticeable amount, a serious amount," Guero finished, putting his beer down with finality. The only people who knew Danny moved that product were dead, and he could easily blame the disappearance on La Familia. Lying to his boss was a risk Guero was willing to take. The deaths Rueben may brush off, but the stolen property he could not.

"I want all of it back." To an uninformed observer Rueben would seem to be talking to himself. But Guero knew to take it as a direct order. "And I want the person responsible dead. I don't care what kind of war you start in the process. It's clear they drew first blood."

"Si," responded Guero, throwing money down on the table and following Rueben as he rose and walked toward the door.

*

On the drive home, Guero stopped off at the La Playa resort, just to make sure the rat had been dealt with. He knew Benicio had been the traitor, double dealing with La Familia. But Guero had another leak, La Playa's bartender, Juan.

Over drinks at the bar, Juan confirmed that Benicio had been dealt with.

"Si, Guero. They shipped him off yesterday, to his mother."

Guero winced. "Did they have to send him to his mother?"

"For traitors, it's only fitting," Juan responded. Guero smiled back, now positive that Juan had no idea he had also been unmasked as a traitor. Guero would do what he did with Benicio. Wait until the right moment, and then take care of things.

"Any news I should know about?" Guero said as Juan moved in to pick up some bills placed strategically on the bar. Juan picked up a glass and pretended to wipe it down. He moved in closer to Guero.

"Benicio was seen with two girls, Americans, the day before he died."

Guero felt his stomach tighten. Was one of them her? The woman on the phone who was systematically destroying his cartel? He waited for Juan to continue.

"I think he took them somewhere, into the jungle, because they never came back."

"Benicio said that?" Guero questioned, weighing the words of a traitor.

"He made up some story, under torture of course, that the girls came to him looking for information on how to run some drugs. Load of bullshit. We knew he was planning on selling them to La Familia. Before we killed him, he told us they were staying with him."

"Are they?"

"Who knows, he was probably lying. However, if they are still around, I will let you know."

Guero had the feeling Juan would also let La Familia know. He would have to watch Juan carefully. Nodding thanks for the beer, Guero departed.

Winding up the drive to his house, Guero thought about the American girls alone in the jungle. Juan had been under the impression they were about to be sold and were probably terrified, scared, lost. Guero felt differently. Those girls, especially the one he spoke with on the phone, were not afraid. They were now on the loose, and Los Muertos had better watch out.

20

The missing gun brought Leigh to an awake, sober state. There wasn't time to do a more thorough search before the Matador and Gia exited the car and threw the back of the Jeep open. Quickly, she checked between the seat cushions beside her. Her heart leapt as she felt the familiar lines of rusted steel. Thanking the heavens, she removed the machete and placed it snugly in the back of her bra.

Exiting the car, she was grateful for the cover of darkness, as a cloud had just formed over an unbearably bright moon. Staring into the back of the Jeep with the rest of the group, Leigh shook her head.

"We have more than will fit in here," Leigh began, looking at the compact space as the Matador put the two rear seats down to make more room. Leigh wondered how they were going to ride back.

"This will have to do; you don't want to take a huge amount the first time. We'll just keep running this across until we've exhausted it. I've done this before," the Matador responded confidently.

Even though it was dark, Leigh could sense his smile. She felt desperately out of the loop. If there was one thing she learned about herself, it was that she didn't enjoy following orders. But her instincts told her to follow along, so she dutifully nodded her head.

Turning, she surveyed the opening of the large cenote, as her eyes adjusted to the darkness. The Matador busied himself behind her, pulling ropes and harnesses out from the back of the Jeep.

"What are these for?" Eva asked.

"Rappelling," answered Leigh, an avid climber who knew the accoutrements well.

"This cenote has a pocket of rock cut out in the middle," the Matador responded by way of explanation, after pausing he continued. "Tourists can only tour the top of the cenote, so the hiding place is virtually invisible."

Leigh couldn't track his movements in the darkness but tried her best to do so by following his voice. Leigh caught the end of his last sentence as she walked back to the Jeep.

" . . . lots of cartels like hiding things here; it's just a question of who owns the territory."

"Who does?" asked Eva, who had stuck close to Leigh since they left the safety of the car.

The Matador did not respond, adjusting the harness to the back of the Jeep, and then walking towards the edge of the cenote. Leigh watched his outline as he deftly eased himself off the edge. Slowly, he began rappelling down. They waited several moments in silence for the Matador to find his way. Obviously, he had been here before. Gia was quiet, which added immensely to Leigh's anxiety.

It was clear the Matador didn't care he was stealing property of a rival cartel, which was a problem. What had Gia told him that made him so calm? He was essentially stealing from his rivals, starting a turf war. Leigh desperately tried to push down her nervousness, but the alarms were everywhere.

Gia seemed more alert than she had been since their first night in Mexico. That couldn't be good. And there was that time they spent together when both Leigh and Eva had been sleeping. Damn.

A shout interrupted Leigh's thoughts and brought her attention to the edge of the cenote. A voice echoed up to the group.

"Ok, I'm sending the harness back up, one at a time."

Leigh took Eva's arm and gave it a squeeze. She would go down first.

*

In the darkness, Leigh couldn't see how high she was rappelling, not to mention how slippery and wet the side of the cenote was. But she remembered how it looked in the daylight. A terrifyingly deep sink hole with a pool of dark water at the bottom.

Edging herself into the blackness, Leigh began rappelling slowly. After a time, she began to see the fuzzy outlines of a small beam of light beneath her. After several breathless moments of descent, she suddenly felt her foot snatched out from under her as the Matador pulled her onto the limestone landing.

Leigh focused on the beam of light emanating from the cave as the Matador steadied her and hastily removed her harness. He had brought down a large flashlight, which was now converted into a small lantern, situated on a white packet. The Matador attached the harness to the rope and gave a yell above, the line zipping up to make way for another descent.

No wonder the cartels fought over this place, Leigh thought to herself, the empty cavern was an excellent hiding spot. It was virtually invisible from the top of the cenote, a naturally occurring pocket created by the steady destruction of rock over time.

As Leigh heard the slow sounds of another rappeller at work, she marveled at the size of the passage. The packets were stacked almost to head height, and stretched all the way back into the darkness of the cavern. She wondered how long this took Danny and his men. They had done a careful job, having assumed it would be here for some time before they returned.

After a few moments, Gia joined her in the cavern. The Matador took the harness off her and cast it aside.

"Where is Eva?" Leigh asked, looking at the two of them in confusion.

"She's staying up there," Matador replied. "How it works is, you pick a packet, any packet." He did so, miming his actions for effect.

"You hand it to the lovely Gia. She puts it in the net, and we lift it up using the Jeep's crane. Eva hands it to me and I put it in the car." He handed the packet to Gia, his eyes alert, beady as a ferret. He motioned at a large net next to him.

"Throw them in here before you send them up," he said, speaking to Gia. Leigh now knew for certain that leaving Gia and the Matador alone for so long had been a mistake. They were working more like well-known associates than hour-long acquaintances.

Leigh was still working out what to do about it when the Matador hoisted himself up into the harness and called out for Eva to activate the crane on the Jeep. Leigh and Gia ignored each other in the intervening minutes before the harness reappeared at the entrance to the cavern. Gia dutifully hooked up the net and called up above her.

"Ready?"

An affirmative-sounding "Yep" came from above. Leigh turned, pulled a packet from the pile and tossed it to Gia.

*

After a time, they got a rhythm going. Naturally, they didn't risk music, but Leigh played it along in her head. Reach for packet and toss, turn and watch Gia catch. Or watch Gia stumble, drop, pick it up, and put the packet in the net. She could see Eva in her mind, removing a packet from the net and tossing it to the Matador. Repeat. Repeat. Repeat.

After an hour, about a quarter of the packages were gone, and Leigh was beginning to disappear into the shadows. After another hour, her arms began to ache, and her measured tosses soon became erratic fumbles. It took a few impassioned yells from above for the girls below to realize they were taking a break.

The monotony of the exercise did not blind Leigh to what was stewing between Gia and the Matador. Leigh figured their plan was to load up everything, and then kill her and Eva before they returned to the camp. That's why they weren't worried about stuffing the Jeep full to capacity. They were going to dump their bodies conveniently into the cenote.

Confident on this point, Leigh only had to wait for them to make their move. She figured it would probably be within the next hour so, at which time the Jeep wouldn't be able to hold much more.

Walking back near the edge, she looked up into the fullness of the moon, now unabashedly visible in the sky. Lighting a cigarette, Leigh felt the pinch of the machete she had firmly slid under her bra, fitting neatly between her shoulder blades. They wouldn't be successful, she thought to herself. Not while she had her machete. Relishing this thought, she took a long drag of the cigarette. As she exhaled, she felt a quick hard shove from behind.

To Gia's credit, she shoved Leigh so hard that Leigh flew outward into the cenote and straight down. This saved her from pinging down the rocky sides on her descent. Halfway through the air, Leigh felt drunk again, as if her head was still out on the ledge, and her imagination was the one falling.

The water she hit at the bottom shattered that idea quite literally. She was very much alive, after making a panicked entry into the water. Not knowing what was down or up, through instinct she emerged, hesitating, as if the ceiling of the cave would come crashing above her. Gratefully, it did not, as she floated face up.

For a few seconds she oriented herself, staring up at the moon, which looked back at her from the lightening sky. Flipping over, she paddled toward the edge of the underground pool, feet searching to determine the depth of the water, the now exposed moonlight guiding her path. Once steadied, she frantically reached for her machete, touching only wet skin. Slowly, she pulled herself up and out of the water, heart racing. One word flashed in her mind.

Eva.

Stumbling in the darkness at the bottom of the cenote, god knows what squelching underfoot, she had thoughts only of reaching the top. As she searched for some footholds, she saw a flash of metal beside her. Reaching along the rocky floor, she grabbed the handle of the machete. Not wanting to risk losing it again, she placed the thin blade firmly between her teeth, whirling around to begin a slow and steady climb up the heavily marked limestone.

After only a few minutes of climbing, Leigh paused to take a deep breath. She felt her lungs straining, her head still spinning from the fall. Each step up brought the sky closer to her. Leigh's hands and feet ached under the sharp rock. She soon had a rhythm going. Step up, look at the moon. Step up again, rest.

Leigh paused, gazing up at the seemingly endless rock ledge above her. Resting her forehead on the rock, careful not to cut herself with the blade of the machete, she allowed herself a moment of despair. She would be lucky if this didn't take all night.

21

Leigh thought the sounds were a hallucination. She must be dead, and the climb her eternal purgatory. Her teeth clenched the machete as if it had become a part of her. Her muscles ached from climbing. But she couldn't deny what she was hearing, an engine running, footsteps, shuffling.

Looking up, the moon was so large in the sky it appeared as if it would topple into the cenote. But it must be a sign. It can't be far now. Step up, she told herself. Look at the moon. As her knee scraped up a rough section of rock, her hand wavered in the open air. This time it didn't fall on grooved rock, landing instead on smooth perpendicular ground. Arms shaking with strain, Leigh pulled herself up onto the ledge. She had climbed to the top of the cenote.

Leigh's ascent had positioned her 45 degrees from where the group had initially descended. Shaking from exertion, she realized she had gotten there just in time. There was Eva, still alive, passing packets to the Matador as they finished loading the Jeep. Leigh pulled herself up to her knees, and waited, keeping her breathing even while she remained shrouded in darkness.

Eva was now helping Gia up onto the ledge of the cenote. As Gia took off the harness she gave a wary smile to the Matador, who turned the flashlight directly at Eva, effectively blinding her. Gia walked quickly behind him, situating the pair directly in front of the Jeep. There was now nothing between Eva and the ledge. Almost sensing the shift in their positions, Eva straightened, holding an empty harness and narrowing her eyes against the glare of the light.

"Where's Leigh?" she asked, unable to hide the quiver in her voice. Almost immediately Gia started giggling hysterically, putting her hand on the back of the Matador.

"At the bottom of the cenote," the Matador responded, giving a small chuckle of his own. Leigh could almost see the greed radiating off him. All that product! And much more still hidden below.

Gia must not have been able to restrain herself from pushing Leigh off the ledge so early into their task. And Eva never suspected that the packets being sent up in the harness were being placed there by one and not two people. Leigh swallowed hard, relieved. Had Gia dispatched Leigh when Eva and the Matador were done loading the Jeep, she would never have made it back up in time.

Eva was now looking intently at Leigh's missing gun, which was now being pointed at her by the Matador. They must have searched the Jeep while we were sleeping, Leigh assumed, now bringing herself slowly to her feet. Gia, in some freakish moment of clarity had been waiting for the right moment.

Thankfully, they missed her trusty machete. Leigh slowly removed it from her clenched teeth with one hand, dropping it to the side in anticipation. Slowly, she began walking towards the Matador, her bare feet soundless as she approached.

"Shoot her," said Gia with a whisper, which she quickly repeated more loudly. "I said shoot her. Shoot her!"

The Matador looked annoyed.

"I fucking will. Will you calm down?"

Gia could not calm down, and she continued screaming at the top of her lungs, pawing at him. The Matador pushed her off.

"Someone will fucking hear you, shut the fuck up and I'll do as we planned."

"I'll do it if you won't," Gia replied, lunging for the gun.

"Like hell you will," the Matador cried, easily avoiding her grasp, and turning to face Eva. Leigh was now directly to the left of the Matador, hidden outside the beam of the Jeep's headlights. She took the machete with both hands, and brought it down, diagonally, across his arm. He was no longer holding the gun.

He stared at the bloody stump now pointed at Eva and screamed. Eva lunged to the ground for the disposed forearm. Picking it up, she desperately tried to pull the clenched fingers off of the weapon.

Drawing back, Leigh aimed the machete at the Matador's neck, and brought it down in a wide arch. The decapitated head spun like a bloody sprinkler before landing with a thud on the top of the Jeep. Gia was now screaming. Eva, having managed to pry the fingers off the gun, was scrambling towards Gia. Leigh's arm shot out and grabbed Eva firmly by the arm.

"No, Eva."

"Are you serious? You are seriously doing this to me now. She's dead Leigh, she's . . . "

"It's almost light; they will open the park soon. Someone will hear," Leigh said firmly, trying to pull her friend back from her murderous advance. "This place will be crawling with tourists."

It took all her strength to hold back Eva, who was trying to shake Leigh off and point the gun at Gia at the same time. Having quickly recovered from her partner's death, Gia turned and started to run. Twisting to one side, Leigh let go of Eva and grabbed Gia's thick, blonde hair. Gia screeched in pain and fell to the ground, twisting violently to free herself.

"Eva, gun down," she said, trying to control the squirming Gia. Eva looked at Gia and back at Leigh, and then slowly let the gun fall to her side. "Get that body into the cenote," Leigh continued, nodding towards the Matador's corpse. "Hurry."

After a few seconds, Eva's eyes came back into focus. Turning, she walked over to the Matador's corpse and pushed it over the ledge with a grunt. Retrieving the Matador's head, she threw it into the cenote as well, watching it disappear into the abyss. Turning, Eva walked to the passenger side of the Jeep, where Leigh was struggling to restrain Gia.

"What else does he have in there?" Leigh asked. After a cursory search, Eva located rope, a carefully folded tarp, and some duct tape in the glove box.

"We must have been totally fucking wasted to not see this coming," Leigh said, duct taping Gia's mouth and binding her hands and feet with Eva's assistance. Eva acknowledged this with a nod, casting a nervous glance around her. Repositioning some packets in the back, they hastily shoved Gia directly behind the front seat, throwing the tarp on top of the pile.

Eva slid behind the wheel, drawing the engine to life. Leigh hastily jumped in before she hit the gas, the Jeep's wheels spinning to life. Just as they were pulling out of the entrance, an official looking car was driving in.

"Go, now!" Leigh cried. Eva hit the gas as the other car tried desperately to turn. They sped onto the highway, following signs for Merida. The car did not follow.

Once safely on the road, Leigh turned to the tarp, which she now lifted.

"Don't worry, friend. I'm all over you now," she said in a low, cutting tone. Gia blinked in response, and rested her head on the packets with her eyes closed. Leigh readjusted the tarp, righting herself in the passenger seat, feeling her aching ribs for the first time.

"Where are we going?" she asked, wincing.

"La Playa resort."

"Why there?" asked Leigh.

"Because there's nowhere else to go," Eva replied succinctly. "And besides, the best place to hide is often in plain sight." She turned to Leigh and smiled.

Feeling exhaustion descend on the car, they rode on in silence. As the large white gates of the La Playa resort greeted them, Eva guided the Jeep along several packed rows of cars.

"Stay here with her, shoot her if she moves," Eva directed after swinging into a parking space. "I'm going to get us a room." Leigh nodded.

"Good thing you aren't staying with her."

"You're right," Eva responded, adjusting her hair in the mirror and applying some lipstick. "Because I would fucking kill her."

Gia shuddered under the tarp in response, and tried to shift her body further away.

"Don't move," Leigh reiterated, as Eva exited the car and walked confidently to the reception area.

*

Eva couldn't risk asking for the room that Benicio had reserved for them. So she tried a different track, making up little story about the hotel losing their reservation. Granted, it hadn't been one of her best performances, but all the money they had taken from Jiménez's office came in handy. After she plopped a fat stack in front of them, no one asked for her passport.

Eva collected the room keys and eyed the bananas placed in a decorative bowl hungrily. She took two, put them in her purse, and went to exit the lobby.

On her way out a man in a dark suit and shirt was entering, holding the door for her in a way that required her to maneuver around him to exit. As she did, he took off his sunglasses. She looked up into clear hazel eyes and light brown, almost blonde hair. Set against bronzed skin, the contrast was starling.

"Gracias," she replied, after he held her gaze for a few seconds too long. Feeling herself tingling all over, she admonished herself for taking too long. Leigh was probably worried.

*

Gia was more than happy to take one very long hit from her stash in exchange for being locked in the bathroom. After her hope of escape had been dashed, she apparently needed the distraction.

136

Leigh and Eva retired into their adjoining suite, where they slept for the rest of the day.

Their rest was interrupted when the maids knocked for turn down service. After shooing them away, Eva went back to the room to find Leigh also awake.

"I'm starving, like literally starving," Leigh said.

"Well, you did climb up a cenote," Eva responded, sitting down in a chair opposite Leigh, who was still rubbing her aching ribs. Leigh paused with some concern.

"Do you think anyone will find the car?"

"We need to move it at some point. It's our leverage," Eva said, folding her legs to her.

"Ah yes, the leverage," Leigh smiled, proud of their accomplishment. Pulling her makeup bag to her, she began applying mascara, cursing as the wand slipped, nicking her eyelid.

"Fuck," she murmured to herself.

"What is that?" Eva sat up.

"Oh, just me, I can't get this lash to . . . "

"No that sound, what is that sound?"

Leigh swiveled in her chair, staring at her bag which was vibrating on the edge of the bed. She quickly walked over and dumped the contents out.

It was Jiménez's cell phone.

"I thought you turned that thing off."

"I did. But who knows what Gia was up to when we were passed out. Should I answer it?" Leigh asked, surprising herself.

"No Leigh, not yet. We have to talk about our plan first."

"I think I should."

"Leigh, no." The phone flashed a few more times before falling silent. Leigh tried to nonchalantly change the subject.

"When does our flight leave?"

"Today's Friday, we are supposed to leave Sunday," Eva responded, turning her attention to updating Joy and Gia's phones, putting some updates on Facebook for herself as well. While she moved from phone to phone, trying to cover their tracks, Leigh sat on the edge of the bed, staring at Jiménez's phone. As if on cue, it sprung to life again. Eva was quick to counter.

"Leigh, we are not answering it. We need to come up with a plan together first. Then you can call," Eva replied, putting the phones back in her purse.

"It's just a conversation," Leigh responded. "I'm just going to tell him we have his product!"

"They can track the phone call!" Eva said.

"That shit's only in the movies, Eva."

Eva sat scowling, unconvinced. Leigh let the subject drop, and watched the phone register a missed call.

"We'll figure it out after we've had something to eat."

"Room service?"

"Bar's more like it. I don't think I can look at a room service cart the same again," Leigh replied.

"Ok, let me pee."

As soon as Eva left, Leigh put the phone on silent and watched, nerves tingling. When the phone silently registered an incoming call, Leigh picked up.

22

"Hello?" Leigh said, trying not to sound too excited. After a few pregnant pauses, Guero answered.

"Still enjoying your stay in Cancun?"

"You could say that," Leigh responded, her chest fluttering.

"I was wondering, you see, because it appears it might be much longer than you had intended."

"Why would you say that?" Leigh said quickly and quietly, hoping to evade Eva. She watched the light in the bathroom turn off and exhaled, soon to be discovered.

"Because I have your passports. Difficult to leave without one."

"We can talk our way out of it."

"Not when I have the police looking for you."

Eva walked back into the room and gave a yelp.

"Leigh!" she hissed.

Leigh held her finger to her lips, and pulled the phone closer.

"I want to meet," Guero said, and Leigh felt her stomach drop.

"For what?"

"Silly girl, the passports."

"You'll hand them over?"

"I'll consider it."

"You'll hand them over and you'll get us out of Mexico."

He didn't laugh evilly, like some villain in a movie. Leigh had the feeling he didn't care so much about the passports. Something else was on his mind.

"You left out the part about a large amount of money."

"I assumed you had remembered from our last conversation."

Eva was now pacing back and forth, visibly upset.

"What do I get?" he snapped back, frustrated she would not agree to his demands.

"Guero," Leigh began, using his name. She felt him pause. "You get your little white packets back."

The rest of their conversation was brief and to the point. They would meet for dinner, that night, 9 pm. Go to the main restaurant at the La Playa resort; ask to be seated with the Smith reservation, party of two. He read off the instructions and briefly paused before hanging up. Eva was furious.

"Now will you admit that you are trying, actively trying to kill us. We had a good thing going we could have . . ."

"Could have what? La Familia is probably out there looking for three girls who took the Matador into the jungle and never came back. God knows what Guero has done trying to find us. We have a Jeep filled to the brim with drugs, which is covered by a fucking tarp in the parking lot of a resort. We have a strung out frenemy who just tried to kill us."

"Dinner, Leigh? You can't."

"Oh, *I'm* not the one going to dinner," Leigh responded, finishing her hasty makeup application. Eva stood motionless for a few moments as her words sunk in.

"No way in hell," exclaimed Eva. "Leigh, you have gone too far."

"You know you get more attention here Eva," Leigh began, as Eva narrowed her eyes in response. "Oh come on. The men like you. They like your looks, they like your cute attempts at Spanish."

"I'm not doing it," Eva shot back, crossing her hands in front of her, determined to be offended.

"Come on, you know how pretty you are. You know how to get a man to do what you want. You've already proved that with Danny, Benicio . . ."

"Ok, stop. Whatever, you're just saying this to get me to do it."

"I'm saying this because I know you can make this work. We need those passports back, we need to work out a deal with Guero, and we need to get the fuck out of here. I'm sick of dealing with this mess and I'm tired of feeling like someone is going to attack us at any moment."

"And all the killing," Eva stated matter-of-factly.

"Yeah, that too," Leigh echoed without much feeling.

After a pause, Eva unfolded her arms, the compliments having done their work.

"Where am I meeting him?"

Leigh, taking a sip of water, hastily pointed out the window.

"The hotel restaurant?" Eva guessed, raising an eyebrow. "He knows we're here?" Her face reddened.

"He didn't say," Leigh responded, brushing it off. "I wouldn't send you if I thought it was dangerous," she continued, trying to distract Eva and get herself ready for a long night of waiting.

"Why do you trust him, Leigh?" Eva asked, resigned but still confused at the connection between the two. Leigh placed her makeup back in her bag, not intending to answer.

"Let's get you ready."

They settled on a short pink dress, one of Gia's purchases on the resort shopping spree. The dress was cut daringly low and fit Eva perfectly. After frustration with the bra lines, they decided on ditching undergarments altogether. Leigh then decided to help Eva create her hairdo.

"Why am I wearing my hair like this again?" Eva asked skeptically. She looked more like a high priced hooker than a sophisticated operative.

"I have a feeling he likes bed head," Leigh replied, teasing it a bit more, and then frowning and toning it down a tad. They finished the outfit off with the obligatory pair of high heels.

"I look like a prostitute," Eva said, pouting in the full-length mirror.

"Well then we all do, because I've worn a dress like that before."

"The hair is too much."

"Yeah, let's take it down a bit."

The new style decidedly toned down Eva's overall look.

"I'm fucking nervous," Eva announced, as Leigh finished another coating of hairspray.

"Tequila, now," Leigh responded, whirling around to look for the minibar. They drank about a quarter of the bottle before Leigh noticed the clock.

"You better go. Keep your cell phone with you. Remember we want the passports and an escort out of here. In exchange, he gets his property back."

"What if he says no?"

"You persuade him."

Eva looked up from arranging her purse and narrowed her eyes.

"I'm not sleeping with him Leigh."

"He looks cute!" Leigh exclaimed, pouring them one last shot.

"The answer is no!"

"Uhhh, fine! Just do your best. If he won't bite, we'll leave here tomorrow, drive like hell for the border and see how far we get."

"What about Gia?" Eva asked, glancing at the silent bathroom.

"I haven't figured that out yet."

"Don't you want to shoot her too?" Eva asked, looking slightly buzzed.

"Strangely, no. I don't."

"Well I did, you wouldn't let me," Eva replied. Leigh didn't respond, sitting on the bed with her arms crossed. She had prepared herself for a night in, eschewing anything but comfy sweats and a tank top. She looked at Eva's appearance and smiled, offering one last tequila shot. Eva took this with a grimace.

Rising, Leigh gave her a tentative hug.

"If I thought I'd have a better chance at this, I'd go myself, you know that."

"I know," admitted Eva, pulling away with a smile.

"And if things get crazy down there, just call. We're in this together. If you go, I go."

"If you go," repeated Eva, "I go."

*

Eva was at the restaurant before she knew it, hating the liquor for making passage through the intermediary stairways and rustic resort paths all the quicker. As she heard the mariachi band and listened to the laughs of the tourists, she felt her stomach tighten, her heart beat faster with excitement and nerves. She wobbled on her four-inch heels slightly before confidently strutting toward the host.

"Smith, party of two," she practically yelled at the poor man, giving the name she was instructed. After announcing herself, she took a breath, attempting to switch from unease to total confidence. By the time she strutted to the table, she was virtually on the attack, ready to get their passports and themselves out of the country.

The host took her through a maze of tables before walking out to a more secluded patio. There were single tables set up, set far apart for couples to enjoy some privacy. She saw the table he was directing her towards. A man in a suit with distinctive light hair was checking his phone.

She could see where he got his name. He looked like a Mexican Ken doll. But not big like Jiménez, this man was leaner. As she approached, the host pulled out her chair with a flourish. Eva looked confidently into those bright eyes, which were not blue, as she expected, but more of a hazel brown. She sat down, smoothing the tight pink dress over her hips. They didn't speak for a few minutes, his eyes burning into her face, and then drifting slowly downward. She felt her cheeks redden, and her stomach churned from all the tequila.

"How old are you?" His first question broke the dream-like state of the moment. He looked down, and turned off his phone. She went from femme fatale to feeling like this was her older, disapproving brother.

"I'm 25," she lied, watching his face flinch slightly.

"You are not 25. I have your passports, remember?" he responded in slightly accented English. Eva felt her face flush again.

"We got those made up; you can put down any age," she replied more confidently, taking the glass of champagne that was sitting in front of her and downing it. She replaced the glass. As she did, his hand shot out and grabbed her wrist. His grip was unforgivingly hard.

"No, you aren't her."

"Yes I am. We arranged to meet."

"It wasn't you I was talking to," he responded, pressing her wrist slightly, making her wince. He slowly released his grip. Guero sat back, looking at her, his mind made up.

Eva slowly felt her eyes welling up. Her cover thrown, she sat back at the table, trying to control her shaking hands. He let her slowly compose herself, his expression softening. Not a single waiter had come over.

"I want to meet her," he said, slowly and softly.

"I am her," Eva began half-heartedly.

"Enough," he snapped back, shaking his head in disapproval. Blinking back tears, Eva opened her pink patent leather purse and pulled out her phone.

"She told me to call her," she explained, his eyes watching every movement, "if anything like this happened." He gave her a nod as she hit the speed dial.

*

Leigh heard the phone ring, immediately knowing the news could not be good.

"Leigh?" whispered Eva's voice from the other end.

"What's wrong?"

"He knows. I don't know how he knows," Eva said, her voice wavering on the other end.

"What? So what, did you . . . " Leigh sat up in the bed, turning the television on mute.

"Leigh, please." Eva's voice cracked a bit, and Leigh's pulse began to quicken.

"Ok, Eva. Give him the room key. You stay at the restaurant, have dinner. I'll come get you when I'm done talking to him."

"Ok, bye."

*

Eva clicked the phone off and looked up at Guero. Slowly, she pulled out the room key and placed it down with a slap.

"Room 1701, Casita"

Without speaking he rose, dropped an envelope on the table, and departed. After a waiter came to refill her glass, Eva straightened and plucked the envelope from its perch.

"Would you like to order, Señorita?" he asked. She didn't respond, peering into the depths of the neatly folded envelope, she spied gold lettering glittering back at her. Their passports!

"No, thank you . . . I'll eat at the bar." Standing, she strode over to the hotel bar, situated near the entrance to the restaurant. There was no sign of Guero, he must have departed directly to the room. Sliding onto a stool, Eva checked to make sure there was no hint of tears left on her face. Thus convinced, she slapped the compact back in her purse, smiling as the bartender advanced. Placing down a napkin, he handed her a menu.

"Thank you, er . . ." she looked for his brass nameplate, locating it just as he introduced himself.

"Juan, Señorita. My name is Juan." Eva looked up at him and smiled, finding the face somewhat familiar. It wasn't until after her margarita she felt her limbs grow limp, her vision beginning to blur.

"Juan," she began, as he watched her from behind the bar, "we've met before."

He was the man who tried to neatly block her exit from Benicio's car several nights ago. Eva felt her panic grow as she realized that his intentions were not altogether friendly. Eva hoped there was still time to get out, and get back to the hotel room.

Moving to grab her purse, she cursed her clumsiness as her

chin hit the bar on the way down. The last thing she remembered was being carefully ushered out the back of the restaurant. And then, blackness.

23

Guero knew the way; this was one of their most luxurious suites. As he walked quickly down the sidewalks, diverting glances from the tourists, he found himself very much looking forward to meeting the woman on the phone.

The passports all boasted pictures of beautiful young women. But one had stood out to him. Her cold grey eyes stared hauntingly back at him from the photograph, her face framed by artfully groomed brows and dark—almost black hair. He knew with certainty that it was this person behind that door.

Silently he approached it, knocking once and after hearing a muffled reply, entering with the key he had been given. Walking into the room, he looked quickly to the right, before noticing movement to the left of the door.

That's where she had crouched, ready to strike like a little lioness. But she did not move. He stood looking at her, amazed to see the woman from the photograph in the flesh. Her eyes were wildly alive, taking in his form with curiosity. She had her arms crossed in front of her, leaning on the wall in a guarded fashion. The sight of him seemed to both interest and throw her off guard. He stood very still for a few more moments, not wanting to frighten her.

He had known what he intended to do before they met. Minutes after they spoke, he knew they had to meet. His mind had taken it past that point. And here she was, standing before him, not really caring about all the events that had lead up to their fateful meeting. What was important was that he was with her.

He slowly took a step toward her, and then another. She straightened, and began retreating backward, straight into the room he had intended on finishing their meeting. Looking gently at her, he could see the wall before him crumble slightly. Whatever she had been expecting, it wasn't this. With a bang she hit the back of her calves on a low table. Leigh winced in pain, causing him to momentarily halt his advance.

Watching her chest rise and fall, he was only inches from her now. Slowly, he reached out and took her hand in his. He felt it relax under his grasp. Raising it slowly to his lips, he felt the heat pulsing through her warm hand.

It wasn't asking much to pull that hand toward him, to bring that body closer to his. To feel his mouth on hers. If she had any reservations about what he was about to do, she did not voice them. She came willingly. And it was everything he hoped it would be.

It wasn't until much later that night that he realized what he had done. He wanted to capture this moment, to hide her away for him to enjoy forever. Taking out his phone, he took a picture of her little form, lightly draped with the white linens of the bed, the early morning light hitting every curve.

Putting his phone away, he rolled to one side to watch her sleep. The fact of the matter was she was 20 and obviously in cahoots with a rival cartel.

Taking his phone with him, he slipped out of bed, keeping an eye on her figure. He had several messages, and as he listened to them, he realized the situation was slowly getting worse. He had to act.

Guero could take care of this easily. He could put one bullet in her head and leave knowing he had done his duty. He could go back to the restaurant, find Eva, and kill her too. He shuddered at this possibility and pushed it out of his mind. Leigh stirred in bed, the covers falling gently away. He took a deep breath and rubbed his temples. How did it come to this?

*

Leigh hadn't bothered to put on anything more alluring. She only had time to place the gun strategically by the door when the knock came. Quickly, she positioned herself to one side of the door, leaning against the wall with her arms crossed. Her weapon of choice would be words. She replied calmly to his knock.

"Come in."

He wasted no time entering, but let the door slide open slowly. When he walked into the room, Leigh felt her heart lift from her chosen vantage point. For a few breathless moments, he looked to the right and she couldn't help but admire his dark, lean form.

The blondeness of his hair contrasted so ominously with his tanned skin. The suit was dark and expensive, similar to those black suits sported by the rest of the hotel managers. But he wore his differently, almost like a second skin. Leigh found her pulse quickening, and steadied herself before she was discovered.

After taking in his surroundings he turned to his left, catching her figure leaning against the wall, and paused. He closed the door behind him and stared at her for a few moments. Leigh felt her heart racing, and tried desperately to steady it. Her arms still crossed in front of her, she felt momentarily paralyzed. He made no movement, offered no greeting.

After a few charged seconds, he slowly began walking towards her. Leigh pulled herself from her position against the wall, and retreated a few steps, cautiously resisting whatever was going on. Her words had left her. Guero was in her room. One of the most dangerous men in Cancun. The boss of all the men she had killed, the voice over the phone.

But this was odd, he wasn't approaching her with intent to kill, there was no menace or threat in his advance. Leigh was so thrown that she jumped when her calves hit a low table and drew a quick intake of breath. She could retreat no further.

He stopped his advance an arm's length away, and reaching towards her, he took her right hand and raised it to his lips. Kissing the inside of her wrist, Leigh quickly realized all past drunken makeouts were clear and different beasts than what was happening right now. She felt heat running through her like a flash fire, her middle pounded. His eyes were very tender, his touch deliberate. After he drew his lips away, she still held her hand suspended in the air, not wanting to let the sensation end. As she did, she exhaled softly.

Sensing the break, he pulled her wrist so the gap between them disappeared. She felt his mouth on her lips, and pushed herself longingly into their kiss. Feeling her desire for him, she drew his head into their kiss forcefully. He complied with this new direction, lifting her gently in the air, while walking swiftly into the bedroom. He settled her down on the edge of the bed.

The maids must have been ambitious that morning; a towel fashioned in the shape of a swan lay smack in the middle of it. Leigh felt it hit her head as he continued his attentions, pushing her up on the bed while he pulled the rest of her garments down and off. After a few delicious minutes, she realized that while she was now completely naked, he still wore his suit.

Pushing herself up to her elbows, she drew him from his current position and began working with purpose on his clothing. In a few seconds he was as satisfyingly bare as she, and after a few more moments she wondered at the feelings and power her body was now under. Their bodies moved together in a tender assault, greeting and welcoming each other at every stage. If this was sex, Leigh thought, while wistfully undergoing yet another wave of euphoria, then what the hell have I been doing since I was 15?

They eventually collapsed from exhaustion. Leigh felt his fingers stroke her hair, and then delicately trace the curves of her body as she lay wrapped in the soft white sheets.

She must have slipped off to sleep, because the next second she was on campus, late for her final test. As she pushed through crowds of people dotting the sidewalk, she noticed a girl forcing through the crowds in a similar fashion. They seemed to mirror one another, hopping over a section of broken sidewalk, and forcing underclassman out of the way.

From time to time, Leigh looked and smiled at her, acknowledging their similar misfortune. The girl, who had long brown hair, and wore the same ironic smile, laughed in response.

They pushed the remaining barriers out of the way, meeting at the entrance to the lecture hall. They took seats next to one another, and as Leigh struggled with an answer, the girl slowly slipped her a piece of paper. Leigh dutifully took down the formula, and completed her test. After she turned it in, she noticed the girl had left. The chemistry teacher seemed to notice her confusion.

"Your sister left. But she's in all your classes."

24

Eyes opening, Leigh kept her body very still, rewinding memories of the night before, her heart beating faster as they returned.

She cautiously lifted herself from the bed, looking over one shoulder. Guero was sleeping, or pretending to, his fine features relaxed against the plushness of the hotel pillow. Leigh slipped off to the bathroom, and when she returned, he was sitting up, awake.

She hadn't bothered to clothe herself, after last night there didn't seem to be much point. He straightened at the sight of her, and when he reached out, Leigh wrapped the sheet around her waist and crouched opposite him.

"No more."

"Why?" he asked, leaning toward her and tugging at the sheet.

"I want some answers first." She pulled the sheet down slightly with a casual smile. One which he returned.

"I returned your passports."

"To Eva?" They held their positions. Leigh was precariously perched on one side of the bed, and Guero, like a cat to her canary, on the other.

"What else do you need to know?" he offered, inching his hand closer.

"Whose drugs are those?" Leigh asked, referring to the mystery packets.

"Mine. Well, used to be. Jiménez stole them from me." Leigh looked at him, putting the pieces together in her mind. He had dispatched Danny that night to take care of Jiménez, and they had walked right into his neat little plan.

"And I stole them back," she responded. Guero looked up at

her, but didn't react, having other things on his mind. Taking the sheet and giving it a determined tug, Leigh fell slightly to one side.

"Where have you been?" he asked, pulling the sheet closer to him, pulling Leigh along with it.

"In the jungle," she said, pulling back.

"With who?" He didn't look at her this time, staring at the sheet and giving it another tug. Leigh fell to her forearms, now only a few inches away.

"Friends."

"Do I know these friends?"

"You might."

"La Familia?"

"This is their territory," Leigh said. Guero shook his head once.

"This is not and never has been their territory." He took both hands on the sheet and pulled, Leigh landed, very ungracefully, on top of him. She gave out a delicate shriek as he yanked the sheet away. He held her close to him and she relaxed, letting his hands wander.

"Who are you, really?" he asked, still unconvinced.

"My name is Leigh, and I'm on spring break," she responded, staring at the ceiling. He lifted his head.

"From where?"

"Phoenix. I go to Arizona Southern University."

"Are you really 20?"

"Yes, how old are you?"

"I'm older."

"How old?"

"Older."

Leigh looked at the small lines on either side of his mouth, the creases near his eyes.

"Not too old," she said. He squeezed her shoulders a bit.

"Did La Familia kill my men?"

She shook her head, playing with the sheets. She felt his eyes on her, and then felt his hand travel downwards. Before they reached the intended target, she looked directly into his eyes.

"I did. I killed them."

His hand stopped, and he returned her gaze, for once, unguarded.

"I killed Jiménez and his men. I killed Danny, and some guy who called himself the Matador. And many, many more."

"Why?"

"Because if I didn't, they were going to kill us," Leigh replied after a momentary pause. She diverted her gaze, and then looked at him once again. He looked at her, unsmiling, but not frowning either. "Are you going to kill me now?" Leigh asked breathlessly, watching him closely.

"You act like you almost want me to," he responded, confused. Leigh didn't answer. Guero bent down and kissed her. It was clear that wasn't the end of the conversation, but neither intended to proceed without getting the building tension out of the way.

After completing that task, Leigh got in the shower. When she finished getting ready, Guero was dressed. He walked over to where she had plopped herself on the bed, intending to apply lotion. He took her face in his hands.

"I'm not going to kill you."

"Why? Don't you have to? Isn't that the end of all of this?" Leigh responded, a little more loudly than she had intended.

"I had set into motion plans for La Familia long before you came along," he responded, kissing her on the forehead. "Besides, killing you doesn't feel right." He turned abruptly and walked out, closing the door to the bedroom behind him.

Leigh wanted to yell back about the drugs, about their trip home, about the money. But all the words left her. She just wanted him back in the bed, wanted to rewind to last night. After a few moments of sitting motionless on the bed, she rose to dress and search for her cell phone. There were a few harried texts from Eva, the last of which came just after her aborted dinner.

*

Back at the manager's office, Guero hastily pulled up a photo of Jose Beltran. An associate of the La Familia cartel, he represented a perfect trade for the age and status of Danny. This would be Guero's retribution kill.

It was his best shot at gaining a clean break to this mess. He was dead if La Familia encroached any more on their territory. With almost all of his men out of commission, Guero felt the pull of his own demise at his feet. If he did not make a statement tonight, he might as well drive the girls to the border himself and claim asylum.

He used his mole in La Familia to learn the date and location of Beltran's next big dinner. They had these every week, in order to keep tabs on the money and staff, and to generally get shitfaced. La Familia had clearly been bolder in marking their territory. Guero was surprised to learn that the next meeting was in Cancun. The voice at the other end of the cell crackled when Guero passed on this little bit of news to his boss.

"In my town!" Rueben yelled, the emotion of his response practically lurching out of the phone.

"I'm going to take care of things tonight."

"Come see me after it's done," Rueben said coldly.

Guero wrote the details on the back of the photo and had a

trusted housekeeper take it to Leigh's room along with his favorite handgun.

Walking to his car, he began to have second thoughts.

What the fuck are you doing? She's 20 years old. You just gave her a death sentence.

Getting into his car and starting the engine, he drove from the reception area and down to the parking lot.

"They will kill her on sight," he said aloud this time, his mind running wild with images. "She'll be lucky if they don't torture her first."

Scanning the cars, he knew what he was looking for. He had noticed the keys on Leigh's side table. The garish keychain was a dead giveaway.

Bingo.

Guero located a red Jeep parked far away from the others, and pulled up next to it. Exiting the car, he walked over to it and lifted up the tarp.

"Jesus," he said aloud.

The Jeep was neatly packed to the brim with white packets. After quickly calling for backup, he had it all loaded into a hotel van. He relayed directions to his crew, then closed the Jeep and removed the tarp that had been covering the stash.

He knew they were amateurs. After one look at Eva, teetering on her heels, it was clear they were in completely over their heads. But coeds from Arizona Southern University? After waiting for the vans to depart, he barked off orders and got back into his car.

Easing onto the highway, Guero made preparations in his head if all did not go well tonight. After a few minutes, he pushed the memory of their night further from his mind. It was too painful to think that it might be their last.

25

Leigh searched the bar and the restaurant. No one had seen Eva. She went back to the room to wait for her when she noticed the small shopping bag on the coffee table. Sitting on the couch, she looked inside.

In it was a very large handgun with a silencer. She pulled this out, looking at the gleam of metal and placing it on the coffee table. Also in the bag was a picture of a nondescript, portly Mexican man with the name "Beltran" written on it. Flipping it over, she noticed what she assumed were Guero's instructions scribbled on the back.

See Juan, bartender, connections on both sides. Tonight, 7 pm at the Monkey Bar, main drag Playa del Carmen.

She put the photo down and shook the plastic bag. Out came a thick stack of paper. She picked up one deposit slip from a wire transfer. It was a transfer to an account in the amount of $10,000. She flipped through the rest of the stack slowly.

Raising an eyebrow, she felt her heart beat faster, her palms begin to sweat. As calmly as she could, she put everything back in the bag, and checked on Gia, who was in the bathtub completely passed out. Leigh shook her a bit to make sure she wasn't gaming her again, and left some food she found in the minibar on the tiled floor. As she reassembled the barricade, she felt a small ball of worry grow. Where was Eva?

*

Eva woke, her mouth incredibly dry and sore. Easing her head from whatever hard surface she lay on, she quickly lowered it due to the splitting headache she had acquired from the night before.

Slowly, she opened her eyes and took stock of her surroundings. The room looked like a hotel suite, but from the residential look of things she was certain she was no longer in the La Playa resort.

She put the rest of her survey on hold, hoping against hopes that there was a bathroom. There was. She drew herself up off the floor attending to that necessary business. Exiting the bathroom, she walked cautiously around the room. While richly appointed, the windows were seemingly glued shut and the side table next to the bed did not have the obligatory phone.

Without anything to do other than sleep, she had put her head on the pillow when the door opened a crack. She recognized the man with the large semi-automatic gun. It was Manuel.

The last time she had seen him was when he had taken her deep into the jungle to meet the Matador. Looking at his menacing gaze, it seemed as if he remembered. And he did not look pleased.

"Get up, Sleeping Beauty," he scowled.

Pushing her along, Eva exited the room, carefully taking in her surroundings. It was clear she was in someone's private residence. The bedroom exited to a long, carpeted landing with doors on either side. A grand marble staircase led down to a large great room, replete with gaudy Mexican art.

Pushed along by her captor, she caught a glimpse of a stately courtyard and a large outdoor patio. There were men in suits surrounding the house, which was obviously heavily guarded. It was clear she was now in the custody of La Familia.

Reaching her destination, she was forced through French doors into what appeared to be an office. Stopping here, Manuel pushed her down in front of a large, ornate desk. She didn't recognize the portly man behind the desk, but she did not like the intense look he was giving her.

Manuel had called him "Señor Beltran" with a subservient nod. She vaguely remembered she was wearing the dress from the night before, which lent little to the imagination. Sobriety hit her like a slap across the face.

"I'm going to ask you, young lady," he began in very bad English, "one question." Eva didn't move, her head pounding, too much in pain for his villainous dialogue. He took her silence for seriousness, and continued, putting together the words in staccato outbursts.

"Where is the Matador?"

"He's dead," she replied, surprising herself with an abrupt offering of the truth. He blinked, and she continued in a flood of words. "Los Muertos. They ambushed us in the Jeep. We were so frightened, we ran back to the hotel we . . . "

Beltran's face hardened. He shouted a few words to Manuel, who quickly exited the room, and Eva belatedly realized that her utterance of Los Muertos and her disheveled appearance had sent them wildly to action.

For a moment, she thought they had forgotten her presence, until an even uglier man with a pistol began shouting at her in Spanish. Eva found herself being quickly hustled back in her temporary prison, feeling the energy of those around her exiting the house with a definite plan of action. She had no idea what she had done, it was simply the first thing that came to her addled brain.

She sat down on the bed, shaking. One thing was for certain—she had to get out of there.

*

It soon became apparent Eva was not just gone, she was missing. What's more, Leigh didn't think Eva went of her own volition. It was too coincidental. She eyed the plastic bag she had left on the coffee table and glanced at the clock. There had to be some connection. Did La Familia have Eva? There was only one way to find out.

Leigh took the photo out from the plastic bag and read the instructions again. Closing her eyes, she focused her thoughts. So Juan was in the employ of both cartels. He could take her to Beltran, her target. Being the bartender, he also may have seen Eva at the hotel restaurant last night.

Breathing slowly, she took stock of her situation. If she killed

160

Beltran, Guero would let her leave. It was the price of freedom, she knew it.

She headed toward the hotel restaurant. There was only one man working at the bar, and his name tag identified him as the man she had come to see. Juan poured her a drink on the house and she began chatting him up. They talked about the beach, partying, whatever Leigh could think of to make her seem as innocent as possible.

After she had established he was working last night, she causally inquired as to Eva's whereabouts.

"We're supposed to tour the cenote together, but that skank never came home last night. I have no idea where she is! You didn't see her, did you? She had dinner with a friend of ours. A tall guy, Mexican but looks white, with blonde hair?" Leigh batted her eyes at him, waiting.

Juan didn't respond at first, and it appeared to her that he was glancing around to see if anyone was looking. Leigh pretended not to notice, taking the shot he placed before her with a grimace. Slowly, he answered.

"I don't think you'll see your friend again, Señorita."

"Oh whatever," Leigh began nonchalantly. "She's probably passed out drunk somewhere." He began nodding in the negative emphatically, throwing off his earlier apprehensions with ease. They were now alone at the bar.

"I saw her last night," he began. Leigh perked up and asked for another shot.

"What happened?"

"She was sitting at the bar and got a message. Message says a friend is here to see her. She leaves, bam. For good."

"But where?"

"She leaves with bad people. You stay here in the hotel."

"I have to find my friend," Leigh responded, wistfully looking into his eyes. He shook his head.

"She is with La Familia now, Señorita. You won't find her."

"Hmmm, in that case I better see about this reward," Leigh replied, breaking the valley girl routine with the brash statement. "Thanks for the drink. And what is your name again?"

"It's Juan," he responded quickly, giving her a double take. "You said something about a reward?"

"La Familia wanted to get their hands on this girl for some time," she said. He raised an eyebrow and Leigh smiled, enjoying his surprise. Swirling the drink, she continued.

"They hired me to find this girl, but she went missing before I could snatch her. Apparently, she killed one of their own, some guy called the Matador. Anyway, I guess the person responsible won't get the credit. Too bad," she said, nonchalantly.

Leigh looked at Juan, eyes glued to hers, sweat beading on his face. "If you ever find out who it was," she continued, throwing the hotel card with her cell phone number scribbled on the back, "have him call me. My name is Leigh."

*

Leigh walked back to her hotel room, checked her messages and waited. It might take him some time, she consoled herself, but Juan would crack. She was now sure that Juan—more specifically La Familia—was behind Eva's abduction.

Watching the silent phone, she slowly pulled the covers toward her and wrapped herself in them. Filled with worry for Eva, she needed some kind of comfort. And the smell of Guero, still clinging to the sheets, sent her stomach spiraling. If she pulled this assassination off for Guero, it might cause enough distraction for La Familia so Leigh could find Eva and get the hell out of Mexico.

Pulling the photo of Beltran off the side table, she looked again on the instructions on the back of the card. The time for her assignation was rapidly approaching. She checked the clock, just after 3 pm, they would need at least 2 hours to get down to Cancun. She massaged her temples, concentrating.

Please phone, ring.

Leigh picked up the photo again and placed it gently down on the covers. Almost on cue, her cell phone's musical ring tone began to play. She drew the phone to her, didn't recognize the number, and answered it.

"Leigh?" the person on the phone asked.

"Who is this?" Leigh replied, anxiety turning to anger.

"It's Juan," he responded, almost hurt. She decided to poke at him a bit.

"And?"

"Juan, from the bar. You said something about a reward?"

Leigh smiled.

"Yes, Juan. I have a gift for you, from La Familia," she whispered it into the phone, feeling his excitement from the other end.

"You really are from La Familia?"

"They put us lots of places," she responded, searching around for Gia's cigarettes. She lit one hastily. "You want your reward? Come to my suite, I'll tell you more."

After reading off instructions, Leigh hastily bathed and put on a flowing maxi dress. Her phone rang again and this time Leigh recognized the number.

"How did you get this?"

"I got tired of calling Jiménez's phone and, besides, I was up for a bit last night."

"So I noticed," Leigh responded, ridiculously thrilled she now had him in her call history.

"You get my package?" he asked, his voice sounding a bit strained.

"I did." Leigh eyed the shopping bag.

"What do you think?"

"I think it's our way out of here."

"Correct."

"How do I get there?"

"What about your red Jeep?"

Leigh's stomach dropped.

"I found your car," Guero continued, filling in the blanks for her.

"Dammit!" Leigh cried, genuinely frustrated.

"That was a lot of product, Leigh, I couldn't let you keep it. Besides, someone else might want it. Some people who would like to hurt you."

Leigh drew the photograph toward her, trying to shake off her disappointment.

"This address, how many people should I expect?" Leigh flicked the photograph for emphasis.

"You are attending a private dinner for a few of La Familia's generals. Everyone in the restaurant is in their pay. Juan will take you; he'll be honored to attend." Leigh paused before responding.

"I know, he's coming over now."

"Call me when you are done," Guero responded. Leigh closed her eyes, trying to calm her shaking hands.

"Goodbye," Leigh said, before he could get in another word.

Changing her mind about her outfit, she found a little black dress and paired it with a tall pair of heels. She planned the movements of that night in her head as she waited.

Find Eva, kill Beltran, and get out of this fucking country in time to actually spend the money she stood to make. But while the previous kills had been justified to abandon, Leigh felt a sense of emptiness as she checked her weapon. This time she had something to lose.

Hearing a knock at the door, she ran over to open it.

"You can't wear that," Leigh teased, opening the door to see Juan in this work outfit.

"For what?" he responded, nervously.

"For dinner tonight, for La Familia's top brass." She pulled him into the room, as his eyes widened.

"A private dinner! I've heard about these, they talk and make plans and . . . "

"And you my friend are invited, but first you have to drop me off at Beltran's place."

"Why?" asked Juan, eyes narrowing as his hand fingered the pants of his uniform. Leigh rolled her eyes suggestively. "Honey, he has needs too!"

Juan smiled in response and Leigh's heart regained its normal beat. She had pieced all the associations together in her head, but it was another thing to have them neatly fall into place.

"So you go change, and I'll meet you in the reception area."

Juan departed as quickly as he had come. He was fast about it. No sooner had Leigh stepped off the curb in the reception area when a black car sped up to greet her.

Juan had changed into the requisite dark black suit, looking very small in it. Leigh opened the passenger door and took her seat, fixing her dress as she did. She placed her purse down on the floor mat, the ambiguous shape hiding the gleaming metal within.

Juan quickly assured her that he knew where Beltran lived, puffing his chest out proudly. As they drove out of the resort, Leigh pondered what life would have been like if she had never had to pee that fateful night. They would probably be on the beach, ignoring each other, waiting for the flight home and the subsequent posting of Eva's sex romp.

The car now gaining speed into their nearly two hour drive, she slowly let go of what might have been, and replaced it with a new feeling. It was as if the world had opened up to reveal new and frightening possibilities, and Leigh realized she fit right in. She was right at home.

Lost in her thoughts, Leigh mentally clocked the minutes before she began seeing signs for Cancun. As they closed in on the city limits, Juan turned off the main road, driving up a steep, private drive.

Pausing at the top, Leigh glanced out at what she assumed was Beltran's home. Slipping out of the car, she winked at Juan and took a cursory tour of the property. The front of the house was gated, and by peeking around the side hedges, she found the back heavily guarded and alive with activity.

Undetected so far, she slipped out her phone and marked the location on her GPS. Hearing movements, she peaked past the hedge again. Many of the men seemed to be preparing to exit, probably going to the same party where she was headed. As the lights went out, one by one, she noticed a room at the top of the structure was still lit. It was a hunch, but it was the best one she had since Eva went missing.

Slipping back into the passenger seat, she gave Juan the go ahead, and they joined the train of armored black cars down the mountain. They proceeded to the restaurant in the heart of the touristy beach town and parked.

Exiting the car and advancing towards the Monkey Bar, Leigh was struck by the shameless tactic. La Familia ingeniously placed themselves in the middle of a tourist trap. Any nerves she had about being discovered were unfounded. There were plenty of scantily clad women, many of them white, gyrating to rap music outside the Monkey Bar.

Leigh was right at home as she walked into the restaurant. The only distinction between her and the gaggles of coeds around her was the gun inside her purse. As they entered, Leigh could feel it slap against her hip with every step. Juan had followed her inside, and was stoically wide-eyed with nerves. She shook his hand and directed him toward the bar, rolling her eyes at him.

"You'll never make it with this group if you look nervous." Leigh had the bartender pour him a stiff drink and patted him on the back. "Have a few more, then meet me upstairs. And you'd better let me have these." As she grabbed the car keys from him, he dutifully nodded, downing the shot and looking straight ahead, petrified. Before Leigh could leave, she was neatly blocked by a very large man in a dark suit.

Leigh's stomach dropped for a moment until realizing the man was looking for Juan. Smiling, the man patted Juan on the back, letting Leigh slip by with a gentle squeeze. Leigh got the impression that while Juan wasn't invited, he wasn't unknown to the cartel.

Moving through the crowd unaided, she didn't see anyone matching the photo. She knew the price out of Mexico was this killing, and she felt her heart thump in anxiety that her target may be absent. Frowning, she did a visual scan of the restaurant before spying a stairway at the back of the bar.

The man who had greeted Juan earlier walked directly to the stairwell, seemingly to guard it. Leigh quickly surmised that this must be the entrance to the VIP section. Moving her body to the beat, she decided to do some quick reconnaissance in the ladies room. Slipping past a few stumbling women, she opened the door to the bathroom.

A few heavily made up women were surveying themselves in the cracked mirrors. Casually, Leigh complimented their dresses, observing how terribly lame the party was that night. They nodded in approval before Leigh continued.

"So where's the real party?" she asked, flipping her hair and shaking it for effect.

"Oh, you mean the Beltran brothers," stated one, adjusting her dress in a manner that didn't suggest much in the way of modesty. Beltran, Leigh thought, the name from the back of the photograph.

"On the roof," responded the other, applying a thick coat of unnecessary lip liner. "But be careful, his wife is here."

Leigh thanked them and turned to survey the bathroom stalls. Smiling at her luck, she noticed the corner stall had an "out of order" sign. Pushing it open, she spied a bucket filled with several rags. Hastily, Leigh removed the sign and ducked into the stall.

Moving quickly, Leigh removed her underwear and took a lighter from her purse. Smashing the lighter with her heel, she dumped the fluid on the preciously small garment. She then threw the underwear and rags in the bucket. She took her gun out of her purse, screwing on the silencer.

"Anyone got a light?" She asked, trying to sound upbeat.

After a snicker, someone passed a fold of matches under the stall. Leigh took them with thanks. Bending down, she lit the tangle of cotton before discarding the matches in the toilet. As she exited, the girls were still applying lipstick, not noticing the curl of smoke rising from the stall.

By the time Leigh made her way toward the stairs, she heard a whoosh, and looked down to see clouds of smoke curling under the doorway of the restroom. There was still time. Leigh got past the first guard easily, as she had seen him before with Juan. He nodded at her in recognition.

Climbing the stairs quickly, Leigh noticed there was another beefy bodyguard at the top. She kept the gun hidden behind her purse as she climbed, watching him move to block her as she reached the top. All he got time to blurt out was a quick "Señorita" before Leigh shrieked one word in her best Gia impression.

"Fire!"

Her high-pitched squeal made the man flinch, and he quickly pushed her out of the way and bolted down the stairs and into the smoke now billowing out of the bathroom. The screams from below had now grown to a fever pitch, and as the bodies began passing her in a frenzied exit, Leigh scanned each face for the one she was searching for.

The rooftop bar was nearly empty by the time Leigh reached it, with only one back table filled with patrons. As she advanced, the cluster of men and one woman seated around it looked confused. A few were asking each other if they smelled something. Two looked similar, these must be the Beltran brothers. Leigh closed her eyes and focused on the picture in her mind. Let's hope it was the right one.

"Fire!" Leigh screamed again. Her exclamation spurred them into action, and the group rose and began leaving the table in hasty, panicked motions. In their confusion, Leigh maneuvered behind the portly Beltran, put the gun to his head and pulled the trigger. He fell down on to the table with a thump, bullet lodged in the back of his head. Leigh turned swiftly, tucking the gun back into her purse, joining the rush of people who were now fleeing down the stairs.

By the time she reached the bottom, the wall and half of the bar area were engulfed in flames. After all she had been through, her adrenaline quickly subsided and Leigh's legs suddenly felt like lead. She stopped cold, staring at the blaze. Standing in a trance for few seconds, Leigh was unceremoniously seized from behind and lifted into the air.

Kicking with shrieks of fury, the anonymous hands gripped her like iron, holding her fast. There was no time for guns now, she thought to herself, as her attacker wrapped her tightly in his arms. Resigned that she was now caught red handed, she let herself go limp as she was carried out of the bar and out into the street. Her eyes glued shut, Leigh prayed her death would be swift and painless.

26

As she felt the humid air hit her face, Leigh suddenly was set on her feet with such force it made her teeth rattle. Slightly dazed, she looked up, as the bouncer gave her a gentle pat on the head, running back into the licking flames to rescue more patrons.

Leigh whirled around, amazed at her good fortune, staring at the orange and red blaze now reaching towards the darkened sky. Turning, she ran in the direction of Juan's car. Grasping at the handle, she could hear members of the crowd twittering in the growing realization that Beltran had been shot dead in their midst.

Starting the car, Leigh hoped the phone would pick up a signal. Hands shaking, Leigh set the GPS for the location she was at only hours before. Seconds later, she had the directions.

As she flew down the street and onto the main road, she had a dreadful feeling that there was not enough time. Pumping her foot on the gas, she veered off the road just after the entrance to Beltran's private drive.

Turning the headlights off, she screeched to a halt in the now pitch black night. Before exiting, she took off her heels, and left the passenger door open for a hasty entry. Leigh began sprinting up the private drive, watching the glowing house get bigger with every push.

Once at the top, feeling her lungs pound with exertion, Leigh followed her earlier path behind the house. Tall bushes were sandwiched next to stone pillars and a sturdy gate. Leigh threw herself at the gate, swearing vehemently after it didn't budge. She was hoping they had neglected to lock it.

She looked at the sliver of space between the pillar and the bushes. Thanking pilates and genetics for her slim figure, she managed to squeeze through the narrow space, the sharp branches digging deep into her flesh.

Walking up to what she assumed was a side door, she was

amazed when it flew open, unlocked. She stopped, taking in the room before her. It was a mud room of sorts, leading into a large, marbled great room.

Leigh walked in slowly, her bare feet soundless on the hard surface. Eerie silence greeted her, the low light of the great room and the Kachina dolls lining the sides made her cringe. She felt a wave of nausea. She had seen this room before, but it had been in a dream. And this was reality.

The room opened up before a grand staircase that led to the second level. At the bottom of the stairs was an inky pool of blood. As Leigh walked closer, the blood turned into a dark, rusty red. Skipping over this, and mounting the stairs with increased anxiety, Leigh followed the trail of red marks on the marble to the upper landing.

There were several rooms to her left and French doors leading to what appeared to be an office on the right-hand side. With no blood trail to guide her, she was wordlessly drawn to the room at the top of the stairs, hoping it was the one she had spotted from Juan's car hours earlier.

Glancing inside, she spotted blood-spattered carpet, walls and surfaces. After a few glances at the amount of blood, Leigh assumed this is where Eva had met her end. Walking into the bedroom, Leigh stumbled into a puddle of blood she had missed by the door.

She gave a little squeak, and caught herself on the door frame, also streaked a sticky red. The room was silent, save for her own panicked breaths. Out of the corner of her eye, she spotted a small pink clutch. It was the purse she had coaxed Eva into using the night she sent her to seduce Guero. Leigh ran over to retrieve it, opening it to find a lipstick and nothing else.

"Eva!" she not so much cried as yelled, screamed, demanded. Her words echoed back to her, with no intelligent response save for the echo. Whimpering now, the sight of all the blood in contrast to the perfect pink patent leather purse, Leigh stumbled out of the bedroom. Walking back to the top of the stairs, she sensed rather than saw someone else in the room. It took a few seconds for Leigh to visually locate him.

He was standing at the bottom of the stairs, and it seemed Leigh's outburst had made him momentarily pause in his actions. The immobile body that was lying lifeless at his feet was marked by the trail of blood from the outside. He had been interrupted while dragging the body into the house. For a moment, their eyes met.

Manuel.

Leigh instantly recognized the man who had taken them to meet the Matador on their ill-fated jungle expedition. The man who she assumed killed her friend. Leigh didn't so much run down the stairs as she flew, skipping several steps, and landing firmly on top of him.

Though obviously wounded, Manuel was stronger, flipping her on her back after getting his breath back and slamming her head down on the marble floor. Through the force of the fall, her purse went skipping away on floor, and Leigh began kicking fiercely at the figure above her, landing kicks at the damp blotches on his coat. The sound of a muffled gunshot stopped her kicking, and she watched him crumple over and fall next to her.

Standing behind him, covered in blood, was Eva. She looked like she had several deep wounds on her chest and shoulder, but she held Leigh's gun as elegantly as Leigh had a few minutes earlier. Holding the back of her head in pain, Leigh struggled to her feet, spinning from the impact on the floor.

"Eva, are . . . how are you . . . "

"We have to go," Eva replied hoarsely, collapsing on Leigh for support. They didn't so much walk as limp for the door. Eva wordlessly opened the gate from the inside—both knowing there was far too much evidence to conceal their appearance at this point.

Holding each other tightly, they stumbled down the drive. Leigh was the first to see the winding headlights moving slowly up the mountain.

"We have to go faster, Eva."

"I'm trying, I don't think I can . . . "

"Faster!" cried Leigh, pulling her friend from a limp to a slow jog. Eva yelped in pain as she put weight on her right foot, almost falling before righting herself, and finishing the small distance that remained to the car.

Leigh secured Eva in the passenger seat, and sprinted to the other side, turning the engine over with a roar. As she peeled back onto the road, she watched nervously for the headlights that would soon appear in her rearview.

After a few breathless moments, she pulled over to the side of the road, watching the cars pull into the private drive and up to Beltran's house. The sound of blood rushing through her head was deafening. Leigh began to put her head between her knees, decided against it, opened the car window and vomited. Eva groaned.

"Stay with me. Stay awake, I can't stand silence right now," Leigh ordered, feeling instantly better. She fumbled for her phone, finding Guero's number in the call log and dialing it.

"Guero," responded the voice on the other end.

"The hospital, I need a hospital."

"What?'

"Did you hear what I said, I need a fucking hospital!"

Eva flinched at Leigh's outcry, and Leigh whispered an apology while Guero offered up a response.

"Right off the main road you'll find the Cancun ER. I'll be waiting out by the entrance in a black Mercedes. Do not go in, just follow me."

He was quick and decisive, and Leigh felt his own confidence fill the void within her. Without another word she hung up the phone, turned the car around, and drove back in the direction of Cancun. She whizzed past the private drive where they had made their bloody exit, but even from the side she could see the house was lit up like a Christmas tree.

Leigh slowed as she found the turn for the hospital, distressed to hear Eva's breathing getting raspy and pained. She saw a dark Mercedes sitting just to the right of the ER entrance. The headlights flickered. She followed the car to the back of the hospital, revealing a small, one-level structure on the hospital campus, away from the main building. The car hastily parked and Leigh followed suit.

Wordlessly, Guero exited his car and opened the passenger door. He gently picked up Eva, with Leigh running to open the door of what she assumed was the cartel's personal ER. She watched Guero take Eva down a long hallway and enter one of the rooms at the end. Leigh could not follow. Shaking, she turned to a folding chair and dropped heavily into it, bringing her knees up and crossing her arms in front of her face.

*

Eva had been alone in the house for a half hour when the trouble started. She knew which one it would be. Manuel. After she heard all the cars drive away, heard the last step exit the house, she searched aimlessly for some kind of weapon in the suite which had now become her prison.

The best she came up with was a comb, pointed at the end for separating and teasing hair. She frowned at the sharpened plastic, which she was sure would snap on contact, but it fitted neatly against her hip, tucked into the side of her thong.

Sitting quietly in the locked room, she felt him moving around the house, hearing his footfalls on the stairs. She tried to get her breathing under control, easing her dress up her thigh to allow access to her only weapon. Thinking he surprised her, he flew the door open, the look on his face one of obvious malice.

"No," Eva said, firmly and clearly. He gave a small chuckle, and was on top of her so quickly she wondered why she didn't tuck the comb in her dress versus her underwear. It didn't matter; his hands were down there in seconds, closing over the comb with a surprised grunt. He yanked it from her thong, looking at it, confused, the pointed end facing his cleft. Eva took two hands around the comb, and pushed, aiming as much as she could at the glistening wetness of his exposed mouth.

She felt a satisfying give, and he shrieked in pain, falling backwards off the bed onto the floor. Eva leapt over him, almost to the door. The next thing she felt was a burning pain down her left side. Stumbling, she looked back to see him pull the knife back.

Eva felt something puncture, and tumbled back onto the landing, bleeding and panting. Manuel advanced on her, blood streaming down his face, the comb still impaled in his mouth. He raised the knife again as Eva fell backwards with a thump. Looking behind her frantically, she grabbed the foot of a lamp positioned at the top of the landing, and swung it above her head.

It didn't do much damage to his head, but he dropped the knife from his hands, which skidded down to the top step. Eva reached for it, and swung it blindly behind her, she felt it stick, looked back, and saw it jutting out from between the folds of his suit jacket.

Manuel screamed, pulled it out, letting it drop to the ground. Eva stood up, shaking, taking the knife again and bringing it down on top of him. His eyes were glazed over in shock. After he stopped moving, she let the knife fall to the ground.

Stumbling down the stairs, Eva realized she was having trouble breathing. She unintentionally slowed her pace, tripping down the stairs, eyes on the door. The door came closer, she was almost there. Almost.

Suddenly, she blacked out. In the next few moments, she realized she was staring at the bushes outside. And she wasn't alone. Staring down at her was Manuel, knife in hand. He grunted as he brought it down. Eva closed her eyes.

"Will she live?"

Leigh finally said the words, lifting her head up and adjusting her dress so it didn't expose more than she could help.

"They are working on her now," Guero responded, staring off at the wall behind Leigh. She took the gun out of her bag, where she had placed it after Eva shot Manuel. Wordlessly, Leigh slid it across the floor to him. Guero stared at it for a few moments, his blonde hair shining in the overhead fluorescent light. Finally he picked it up and secured it back in his holster.

"Did anyone see you?"

"Everyone saw me. Wasn't that the point?"

"No, I meant getting Eva out."

"The only one who did is dead."

They sat a few more moments in silence.

"I want to go home," Leigh said. By the tone of her voice it sounded as if someone else had said it. Maybe it was Gia, or Joy. But it wasn't her, it wasn't Leigh. She certainly didn't feel like Leigh. She hadn't since she set foot off that plane.

"Home?" Guero responded, with an expression Leigh couldn't quite put her finger on. "You want to go home. Huh? You've had enough. You've done enough partying, got a good tan."

It was anger, Leigh realized. He was angry. Guero shook his head, continuing.

"Go home Leigh. Go back to school. Forget this place."

"I'm just done with this." Leigh shook her head, trying to explain. She snapped off the words, not knowing how she felt, feeling the burn of his anger. "This isn't who I am." Trying to convince herself, she wrung her shaking hands in her lap.

"This isn't who I am," she repeated again. Her ears were buzzing, the sound heightened in the silence of the hospital corridor. Guero didn't respond. They sat there, silent, for a few more moments. Then his phone started ringing. Rising, he left to answer it. At the same time, a thin woman entered from down the hall and began speaking to Leigh in Spanish.

"I don't . . . wait. Guero!" she yelled out at him. He entered, spoke to the woman, and looked back at Leigh.

"She'll stay here tonight. You want me to take you back to the hotel?"

Leigh only had energy to nod. Leading her to his car, she climbed in, enjoying the dead silence of the nearly two hour car ride to Merida. Finally, Guero pulled in front of her room at the La Playa resort.

"It's safe for you to stay here, we are watching you now," he said, looking straight ahead. She looked at him, and when he wouldn't meet her eyes, she exited the car and walked up, shoeless, to her room. She did not even bother to check on Gia.

*

After a long, hot shower, Leigh peeked out the curtains to see his car still sitting there. She held the phone in her hands a few more minutes before calling him.

"I want you to stay here with me. Tonight."

"Ok," he replied, sounding more tired than anything. Leigh anticipated his footsteps and opened the door. After entering, he sat on the edge of the bed, running his fingers through his hair. Leigh took her place behind him, lying down to rest her aching body. After sitting there motionless for close to an hour, he finally turned to look back to her.

"I want to stay with you Leigh, all the time. Not just tonight. I want you to stay with me forever."

"So do I," Leigh replied, blinking away visions of graduating college, growing old and spoiled in Paradise Valley, leading a normal life. Because that really was what it meant, being with someone like Guero. No more apartment on Mill Avenue, no more bar crawls. No more going home. This would be home.

She sat up on the bed and slowly pulled him down to her side, moving on top of him initially to rest against him. Before she could, he took her head in his hands and brought her mouth down onto his. The stress of that night only enhanced their affections, and Leigh imagined the power of their movements somehow meant she could will everything else to normalcy. Eventually, Guero put her gently to his side.

"You need rest, not more activity."

"I've been waiting for this a long time," she responded, watching his features relax, moving closer to a dreamless sleep.

"For what?" Guero asked, placing an arm around her.

"A home," replied Leigh, pulling herself closer.

27

Leigh woke the next day feeling like someone had slammed her head on concrete. Sitting up, she remembered that someone had. Guero was on the phone, looking tense. He turned it off and walked over to her, moving the sheets around her and placing a kiss on the top of her head.

"I'm leaving now to check on Eva."

"When can I see her?"

"As soon as she . . . if she wakes up," he carefully said. "I have some more bad news," he continued, trying not to be cryptic but failing.

"What," Leigh asked, feeling more awake.

"Your actions last night had the desired effect. But it seems someone informed my boss of your activities." He eyed her meaningfully, and then continued. "It might delay your trip home." Leigh felt a flush of warmth, her stomach tighten into a knot.

"How . . ."

"It's up to him at this point."

"Are you going to tell him the truth?"

Guero came as close as he could to grinning.

"What do you think would happen to me if I told him that two college girls came here on spring break, killed all of my best men, and stole from me?" Guero began busying himself with arranging the sheets around Leigh's feet.

"So he thinks La Familia is responsible?"

He nodded in the affirmative.

"Does he know about . . . ?" Leigh let the question drift off, gesturing to the both of them with a smile.

"About us? Probably. Everything else you've conveniently misdirected, placing the blame on La Familia. Now that you've killed my equivalent, it will send a strong message. Let's just hope Ru . . . " he stopped himself, and then continued, "my boss buys it."

"What about me? What about Eva?" Leigh asked.

"I don't know yet," he responded truthfully, "but I'll try."

"Lucky for me I'm so good at killing people."

"I would like it if you hadn't killed anyone, then I wouldn't be in this mess."

"But then we wouldn't have met," Leigh responded, kicking the sheet off her and stretching. She lowered her eyes. "Do you have to leave right now?"

*

While Leigh was in the shower, Guero gave serious thought to locking her up in his house. He thought about it for a good five minutes before he knew it would never work. She would break free from whatever elaborate prison he would fashion for her, probably killing him in the process. No, Leigh would have to take the first step to come to him. It wouldn't work otherwise.

He wondered why she said she wanted to leave, when it was so obvious to him that her home was here. It must be some misplaced loyalty to Eva. He knew they were more alike than dissimilar. This must have been an unsettling revelation for her. Holding his phone in his hands, he weighed calling Rueben, admitting everything. Dialing the number for his boss, he hastily changed his mind.

"Sir, I have good news."

"Does it have to do with a restaurant fire?" Rueben responded, in a good mood. So he had heard.

"Yes, I have some answers for you as well," Guero said confidently.

"Come tell me in person." Rueben kept things short and sweet.

For a second, Guero wondered if this had another meaning, but pushed the thought away. He pulled it off this far, he genuinely hoped they could take it one step further.

*

After Guero left, Leigh got dressed and ate something. She sat down on the sofa, and turned on the television. As soon as she did, she regretted not doing so earlier, as the first thing she saw was a picture of her, Gia, and Joy at last year's rock-n-roll marathon.

They had gone to cheer on their partnered fraternity, and were in matching tank tops, short shorts, and university garb. She felt her throat tighten. So the secret was out. A few seconds later Gia's father was on TV, pleading for his little girl's return. "Never Returned From Spring Break," the headline said.

Had they missed their flight home? Leigh couldn't think straight. She flipped through her purse to find their reservations. Grabbing them in her hands, she hastily compared the details to the date that glowed on her cell phone.

They should have walked off the plane yesterday around 3 pm. Eyes glued back to the television, she watched the taut expression of Gia's father as he faced the camera. She felt the blood drain from her face as he continued talking.

He had waited and waited at the airport for Gia to arrive, only to watch them clear out the plane without his daughter. The hotel was claiming the girls never arrived. Mexican officials were saying there was a problem with his passport. He hadn't yet been cleared to come into the country. He thought that something terrible was going on . . .

Leigh watched with increasing horror. They had to get back. Had to. Before he came down here, metaphorical guns blazing. She was sure someone was behind the convenient passport debacle, or else Gia's dad would be down here by now. He had some serious connections, it was only a matter of time before he arrived.

She scrambled around the suite, grabbing clothing and makeup and throwing it in her duffel bag. She went to the bathroom, disassembled the barricade, and threw open the door. Gia was awake, cowering in the bathtub. Miscellaneous bits of food were strewn about, but it didn't appear she had eaten any.

"Come on, we're leaving," Leigh shouted out the words as she flew into the bathroom, grabbing Gia's arm and hustling her into the living room.

"Pack your shit, you have five minutes." Leigh took a handgun from her duffle bag, and stuck it firmly in her the band of her skirt. Gia had placed a few items in a bag before Leigh grabbed her arm and took her down to the car. She had ditched Juan's car at the hospital but didn't ask what Guero had done with it. Besides, he had left her his Mercedes. Leigh opened the trunk.

"Get in."

"You have to be kidding me," Gia spat, still incoherent.

"Get. In." Leigh cut off the words one by one, her pulse racing, feeling the steel of the gun pressing against her stomach. Gia's father was incredibly wealthy and powerful. Leigh had no qualms that he would have her buried in the foundation of his next subdivision if he found out what his little girl had faced in Cancun.

Sensing Leigh's mindset, Gia crawled into the trunk. Closing it firmly, Leigh drove the two hours back down to the hospital.

Arriving at the same location she had left Eva the night before, Leigh brought the car to a halt. The structure was locked, but with enough banging, it was opened by the same woman from last night. As Leigh hastily entered, the woman followed her down the hall, complaining in Spanish. She gave up and tried a few English phrases. Eva was still hurt, she tried to explain. She should not be moved.

Leigh walked into the door at the end of the hall and entered. Eva was awake, her dark brown eyes pained but coherent. The nurse stood behind her, startled at her patient's powers of recuperation. Leigh took a few tentative steps into the room.

"Eva. We have to leave . . . we are all over the news."

"Who is?" Eva responded, slurring her words a bit. Leigh eyed the drip, which she assumed was morphine.

"We are," Leigh replied, watching the realization on Eva's face.

"What are we going to do?"

"We're going to drive. Now. We are going to take you home."

Eva nodded, pulling her legs to the side of the bed and pausing for a moment.

"We need pills," Leigh explained to the nurse. "Pain pills. Eva." Eva turned and said a few words in Spanish. The nurse tried one futile attempt to make them stay, but one look at Leigh and she turned resolutely.

She returned with a bottle of pills, using a series of gestures and fingers to relay dosage information. Leigh dutifully tucked them into her purse. Eva dressed as quickly as she could, considering she was doped up, putting on a white tank top, sans bra, and Gia's Arizona Southern University shorts that Leigh had brought from the car.

Helping Eva to the car, Leigh eased her in the passenger side once again and shut the door. She passed the front of the car to the driver's side, and as she did the nurse crossed herself. Leigh paused, and looked at the woman, frowning. She looked back at Eva, her eyes closed with pain. Getting in the car, she reversed, turned on the GPS, and started driving like hell for the border.

28

Guero adjusted his suit collar, preparing to beg for the lives of his girlfriend and her friend. He couldn't avoid thinking of her as that. His girlfriend. From the earliest moments together, before her body moved next to his. He knew.

His boss, unfortunately, would not see things quite that way.

"Danny" was the first word out of Rueben's mouth. Danny was a relative and Rueben had to ensure his death was avenged.

"Avenged last night," Guero replied.

"On the main strip! The tourists must have shit!" Rueben said, almost amused. "Who did you use? I thought they killed almost all your best men?"

"I had someone on the inside," Guero responded. Rueben accepted this with a nod, taking a photo from his pocket and throwing it on the table between them.

"Who are they?" he asked, glancing down at a picture of Leigh and Eva, exiting Guero's Mercedes on the way to the ER. Guero mentally chastised himself for being so careless. They must have been followed.

"They got mixed up with La Familia," he began, keeping his pulse in check. "They are Americans, on vacation. One of them picked the wrong boyfriend at a bar, got beat up."

"And you helped them?"

"They helped me with a few things."

"So I see," Rueben responded with a smile. He tapped on the photo. "Where are the other two?"

Guero didn't respond.

"I've been watching the American news this morning," Rueben continued. "One of the girls has a father causing all sorts of havoc." Rueben was now running his hands through his thinning hair. "I made some calls, so he's not coming our way anytime soon, but these girls are going to have to be dealt with. I can't have this father snooping round my resort."

"The best way to do that is to take them home," Guero responded, hoping he didn't seem too impassioned. Rueben shook his head.

"They can't leave now, not after this." He pointed again at the photo. "Word gets out—it's not good for business. You make them disappear, ok?"

"Like I said, these girls are American."

"So, we blame it on La Familia. We say it was them."

"These girls are different."

"How? You aren't making sense. You feeling ok? Getting enough sleep?" Rueben looked at him pulled out a cigar, patting each side of his jacket in search of a lighter.

Guero pulled out his own lighter and lit Rueben's cigar. Smoking always relaxed Rueben, and Guero was hoping it would have the same effect on his decision making. Still, he didn't want to push his luck, so he changed the subject.

"I recovered the product."

"Excellent!" This put Rueben in a good mood and they joked for a few minutes on what an idiot Jiménez was.

"Did I tell you he slept with my ex-wife? The bastard. Found out from her, she waved it around in front of me. But I cut ties with that bitch, she can do what she wants. Did I tell you what Jose told me about . . ."

They gossiped a bit. Guero had no idea why Rueben would stab a man in the eye for looking at him the wrong way, but trusted Guero so completely. If he chalked it up to anything, Guero assumed it was he knew when to talk business and when to leave things alone. He took care of problems before they became problems. Well, until now. He half listened as Rueben continued rambling on.

". . . said the rash was going to go away, but it hasn't. I should probably see that fucking quack in Cancun but he charges me double. "

Rueben suddenly switched gears, as he was often wont to do.

"So. You got all of the product back?"

Guero nodded, lighting his own cigar with a steady hand.

"How did you get it?"

"Remember those girls?"

"What girls?"

"Those girls, the Americans."

"Yes."

"They got it back for me."

Rueben was silent for a few seconds, staring past his cigar with an intent look on his face.

"Where are they now?"

"I had them followed," Guero admitted, feeling a flash of guilt for neglecting to warn Leigh. Still, he knew she wouldn't sit still for long. And he knew she was protected if he knew her whereabouts. She must have been driving all day, through the night, and into the next day. He tracked her an hour south of the border.

"They should be close to the border by now."

"I want to meet them."

Guero nodded, making a quick call to arrange for the helicopter. They rose to leave directly, and as Guero opened the car door for his boss he mentally prepared himself for a standoff.

*

After driving nearly 24 hours straight, Leigh pulled off the highway. There weren't rest stops in this part of Mexico so much as there were random pull offs. Eva was passed out in the passenger seat. They had traded off driving, even letting Gia out of the trunk to pitch in—they had no choice.

But no one would be served by dying in a crash due to lack of sleep, so Leigh pulled off the road with the intention of taking a 15-minute cat nap. She was just settling herself into the seat when her phone rang. Leigh put it on silent and slept for what seemed like a few minutes, but when she awoke again the phone glowed with unread messages, and it had been several hours. Finally, Leigh returned the missed calls.

"Where are you?"

"I'm in the desert, a few miles from the border."

"Please stay there." Guero sounded very concerned, not tense and stressed like he was before. With a hint, a tiny hint, of anxiety.

"I can make it," responded Leigh, her voice cracking from lack of sleep.

"No, you can't," Guero corrected. "He wants to meet you."

"We're not going back," Leigh replied.

"Leigh. . ."

"You know where we are, you can track this phone call. Come to this location in two hours, we'll talk about it then," replied Leigh, fully intending to be across the border by then.

"Leigh. We're already here."

Leigh felt her heart drop. Squinting in her rearview mirror, she made out a line of cars appearing behind them. She turned off the phone, feeling stillness fall around her. Of course he had her followed. How stupid of her, she should have known.

Turning to Eva, still sleeping in the front seat, she gently shook her awake.

"Eva, wake up."

"Mmmm," responded Eva, wincing with pain.

"Get up, Eva," Leigh whispered, trying to hold back the tears that were beginning to well inside her. Eva opened her eyes, and turned her head. She looked at the cars for a few moments. Lined up in a row, they shined like tiny black beetles in the afternoon sun. Turning back to Leigh, she sighed.

"Is this it?"

The nonchalance of the response hardened Leigh's resolve.

"Yes."

Leigh's sadness slowly shifted to anger. The way it had that fateful night of the party, when she had snapped into a million pieces. They watched as several men slowly piled out of the cars behind them. Leigh followed their lead, motioning to Eva to exit the car. They walked out behind the Mercedes and waited.

29

Leigh felt the gun pressed against her waistband, belatedly wondering if Eva was likewise armed. There were 10 men in all, and they advanced on their position for several paces, stopping only a few feet away. Guero stood off towards the right, meeting Leigh's gaze with an assured, confident look, not at all betraying his tone of a few minutes earlier.

"Señoritas," spoke the man Leigh could only assume was the boss. He was much older, around 60 or so, shorter than Guero, but with eyes that were cold and serpentine. He swallowed, made sure his men were at ease, looked at Guero hard, and continued. "I'm afraid you cannot go back home."

Leigh shook her head and Eva offered a small grunt.

"We are going home. Today," Leigh said, as clearly and pointedly as she could. The boss looked down at his ringed fingers, now folded in front of him.

"You will come with us. Stay for a while. You like resorts? We have them here. You stay with us for a bit, and then we'll let you go."

He let the demand hang in the air. Leigh, despite being charged from the confrontation, was exhausted. She felt her knees beginning to shake, and couldn't help stealing glances at Guero. After a few moments, she felt Eva stiffen beside her.

"I have a proposition," Eva said, her voice clear as a bell. Leigh looked at her, wondering if the morphine hadn't gone to her head. Eva shifted position to ease the pressure on her arm, which the nurse had put in a sling. The boss kept his eyes down, though Leigh felt a spark of interest in the negotiation, where previously there was merely annoyance.

"We are all over the news," Eva continued. "It only makes sense to give the Americans a happy ending."

The boss let her finish and then gestured with his hands. Go on.

"Let us go back, and tell our story. How we were kidnapped by La Familia on spring break."

"How do I know," he responded, growling back at them. "How do I know that's all you'll say?" Leigh shot a glance at Guero, who slowly nodded his head. Whatever this meant, she was reassured. She could feel Eva's strength beside her, even as her own faded into the brown dust now swirling around them. Eva nodded.

"I was thinking about that," she shouted back. "I have something for you. A gift for you, to keep us honest." The boss looked over at Guero.

"Watch her," he grunted. Reluctantly Guero took out his gun, and let it rest by his side. The other men shifted, visibly alert.

"Open the trunk," ordered Eva. Leigh turned, looking at her with slight confusion.

"Open the trunk!" Eva shouted, her voice ringing once again with clarity. Leigh walked over to the car, opening the trunk to reveal a startled Gia. Eva joined Leigh at the back of the car, and grabbed Gia by the hair with her good hand. Leigh stood to her side, not fully understanding the direction of the negotiation. Eva pulled Gia to her feet, ignoring Gia's screams, and dragged her to the line of men. Forcing a panicked Gia to her knees, she faced their opponents.

"You take her," she hissed at them as Gia's shrieking reached fever pitch. "I said take her!" she screamed, shoving Gia to the ground. A slow and wicked smile crept along the boss's face. He began chuckling, which slowly turned into a full blown laugh.

"Señoritas, I bow to you." The other men were laughing now, eyeing a shaking Gia with excitement.

"Proposal accepted!" he cried, and his men descended, grabbing Gia and forcing her into one of the cars. She was pulled into the dark interior, her screams muted with the slam of the car door. As the men began piling back into their respective vehicles, the boss slowly approached, taking Eva's hand in his and kissing it.

"Till we meet again, Señorita."

"I think not," replied Eva. He laughed, gave Leigh a curt nod, and turned to walk back to the car. Guero opened the door for him and closed it, walking to the driver's side before pausing. He looked at Leigh for a few moments, opened the door, and got in.

Wordlessly, Eva ushered Leigh back to their car. While Leigh would have driven, Eva stopped her.

"You drove all night."

"You are hurt Eva."

"I've never felt better in my life. I won't drive long."

"I think we are going to be escorted," Leigh responded, getting into the passenger side and closing the door behind her. They watched the car Guero was driving pull in close behind them. Eva settled behind the wheel and began the last stretch of their journey. After a few moments of silence, Eva glanced over at Leigh.

"Did you at least get a kiss goodbye?"

Leigh didn't answer immediately. She studied the stitching on the passenger handle, trying to get her head around her feelings. Deciding not to raise the emotional temperature, she turned to her friend.

"I got more than a kiss."

Eva laughed out loud. "Please tell me, I totally need this," she giggled.

Leigh laughed, and started where she left off.

"As soon as you called, I knew something was wrong . . . "

*

Before entering Texas, they left the car in line to enter the United States. Standing a few feet away, Leigh watched as Guero's men took possession of their vehicle, and with it their weapons, their cell phones, everything. She watched as Guero's car then turned, and sped off in the other direction.

Watching the dust rise behind him, Leigh and Eva walked towards the pedestrian entrance, cutting in front of the objecting crowd. Leigh didn't realize how relieved she felt when she saw the American faces. They had been looking for them.

30

Guero drove directly to the hotel to pick up an unsuspecting Juan. To thank him, Guero said, for all his help. On the way to the Cenotillo cenote, Guero cradled Leigh's machete, which his men had brought him after searching the Mercedes she had driven to the border. Guero let his attention draw to the conversation at hand, fighting to keep images from his time with Leigh at bay. He had been talking to Juan about resorts.

"See that's what La Familia wants, they want my resorts. But they don't understand what it takes to work in the world of hospitality." He paused for emphasis before continuing. "Take Rueben for example. He has a way with people."

Juan was nodding, the tiniest bead of sweat appeared on his brow.

"He relies on us as soldiers. Relies on our loyalty, trust. It doesn't work when there is no trust Juan, just ask Rueben's ex-wife."

"I've been loyal, haven't I, Guero?" Juan asked.

"You dare defend yourself to us? You think we don't come to you prepared? You think we are fools? Almost all of our men were killed."

"But we didn't . . . "

"Lies. I won't listen to them anymore."

The car stopped. Without a word, Guero pulled Juan out and led him to the clearing ahead of the cenote. In his right hand, Guero held the machete.

"Such a perfect weapon, the machete. Where its user has complete control." With a slash he sliced off Juan's fingers, who yelped like a beaten dog. Guero paid no mind, entranced by the whooshing blade.

"And while we love our guns, we neglect the humble machete." Another thwack, and Juan's right arm hit the ground with a thump. Guero looked at his watch. The girls would be in custody now, on the other side of the border.

"It's a beautiful instrument. You don't deserve it." He then deftly pushed Juan over the ledge, alive.

*

Juan fell to the bottom with a splash, turning his head from the water, moments away from drowning. After a few breathless moments, he was able to right himself. Paddling to the edge, he hoisted himself up with his mangled hand. Though still daylight, the cenote was completely dark at the bottom. Blackness surrounded him.

Down from above, a beam of light fell towards him, falling a few yards away with a thump. Guero had thrown him a flashlight. He scrambled to pick it up, only to remember his right arm was missing, the blood now leaching from his side like a flood.

He managed to grasp the flashlight with what was remained of his left hand and looked around. He was standing on a foot. As he adjusted the light, he saw the head of a man with a goatee below him. His bloated body was nearby, skin peeling off, Hawaiian shirt still intact.

Juan began vomiting, the flashlight uncovering the horrors around him. There were rotting corpses, skeletons, and, of all things, a large quilted bag, soaking red with blood. He collapsed, letting the flashlight fall from his side. There was no way out.

31

Leigh was sure she was dreaming. Positive. But that didn't seem to matter much. She was sitting in a courtroom behind people she had never seen before. Her father and mother were nowhere to be seen. But she was there with a purpose. There was the judge. There was a man sitting in orange prison garb. She could see the words *Department of Corrections* stamped on the back of the uniform. But she only saw the back of his head. The judge looked at her and nodded.

She rose, making her way to the position just to the right of the judge. She held up her hand and gave an oath, sitting down in the chair and adjusting the microphone. When she looked out towards the crowd, the faces were blurry, but she had the feeling that her family and friends were there. She cleared her throat and looked down at a prepared statement. She didn't read so much as she spoke from the heart.

"I am here today," she began, "to tell you about my sister. And to speak to the person responsible for her death." She stopped, feeling the veritable pin dropping in the courtroom. "I had a statement, I had things I wanted to say. But last night, I had a dream about my sister." She felt the interest in the room shift. Clutching the blank piece of paper, she continued.

"In my dream, we were sitting together on campus, talking. She looked older, not like she was when she went missing all those years ago. And I asked her, what should I say today? What should I say to the person who took her from me? And you know what she said?"

The courtroom was now outside, the sun was shining, Leigh felt the dream ending. But she had to keep speaking, as the realization of her dream and the melting scenery around it brought her own awareness and consciousness.

"She looked at me and said, 'Kill them. Kill them all, Leigh.' "

*

The bright light finally woke her, and Leigh opened her eyes to the fluorescent bulb above.

"So a dream within a dream, huh," she said out loud, then laughed. She was in a holding cell but it was not locked—she was waiting for her family to arrive. The past three hours were a blur.

They were examined and questioned until the police verified their stories. The time Eva and Leigh had spent going over and over the details in the car had helped. When the police sat down with Leigh, lighting her cigarette for her with a look of genuine pity, she knew it had been a waste of time. These guys didn't stand a chance.

*

Eva's experience was eerily similar, and she was almost upset at the total and utter lack of suspicion directed towards the two of them. Sitting with a Diet Coke in an interview room, she relayed the story bit by bit, wincing at the pain of her shoulder.

"It was right after we arrived. We met them on the beach," she began, taking a long drink and continuing.

"We partied. They seemed like normal teenagers. They told us they were with the cartels, sure, but we just figured they were trying to show off. It wasn't until . . . oh God . . . " The baby-faced agent sitting to Eva's left held her shoulder in sympathy.

She gasped, letting a tear escape from her lashes.

"It all happened so fast."

*

"They took Eva into the room first," continued Leigh, taking long drags of the cigarette, and shaking. "When we asked what was going on, they played dumb. That's when the guns came out." Leigh looked up to her rabid audience.

"She probably won't tell you this part, I wouldn't if it happened to me. We all heard the screams. From that point on, they never once stopped watching us. They killed Joy that first day. Threw her in a duffle bag, the pigs. We left the hotel that night, they threw us in the back of the van . . . "

*

"For days they held us in that little hut," Eva said. "It was definitely in the jungle somewhere. They offered us drugs, they, they used us." Eva let the tears fall quicker now. She wasn't sure if she was truly faking it, recounting the moments in her head she was with Jiménez. She decided to go with it and have an all-round breakdown.

"I was so miserable, I thought we'd never escape," she gasped, the tears flowing freely now. "On the last day they took Gia."

*

"We never saw her again." Leigh looked at her interviewer.

"Her dad said she updated Facebook," one policeman said, almost reluctant to interrupt her story. Leigh nodded.

"They made us do Facebook updates, they didn't want people to come looking for us."

"Did they ever say what they were going to do with you?" another asked. Leigh shook her head.

"It was only too clear. They were going to . . . to sell us."

One policeman, so enraged with the story, flipped up his chair with a shout. For a moment, Leigh was genuinely surprised at his outburst.

"I did get a look at their faces though," Leigh offered to the enraptured room, adjusting the thick blanket around her pitifully. "I could identify them."

*

"I think they were planning on killing me. I wouldn't get as much money as the white girls." Eva bowed her head.

"They moved me to a private residence, there was a man with a cleft palate," Eva stated. "He came to kill me. I took my comb, stabbed it in his mouth. He stabbed me, left me for dead. They came back with Leigh. They were angry, I could hear them arguing. I had just enough strength to grab the car keys off the table." Eva's eyes grew wide, as if re-living the terror.

*

"They were fighting, and for once, not watching me. I saw Eva at the door." Leigh pulled the blanket back down, exposing the delicate curves of her shoulders. "We made our move, escaping that night. We used the GPS and drove like hell for the border," she finished, sobbing silently.

"The important thing is that you are alive," the policeman responded, squeezing her shoulder, touched to the point of tears.

"Thank you," Leigh responded, forcing a smile.

There were more questions, of course. A bureaucrat from DC came down to interview Leigh and Eva, though he looked more at his Blackberry than he did at them.

He had outfitted a small conference room with a large interactive screen and they began flipping through the pictures, asking them to identify anyone they recognized.

"Him. Definitely him," Leigh cried, as a very familiar, portly man appeared on the screen. She tried to keep her pronouns in the present.

"I think he is some kind of boss."

"La Familia," one policeman muttered, flipping to show them more photographs. Manuel appeared on the screen. Eva almost flew out of her seat, no acting required. She started shaking after indicating it was, indeed, the man who kept her captive. Eva was therefore distracted when Guero's face appeared on the screen, but Leigh couldn't help but flinch. One policeman nodded his head in the negative.

"Take this one down, he's not La Familia."

"Sorry, he must have slipped in there," another replied, flipping past it. Leigh lowered her eyes, fighting back the lump in her throat. As the interviews concluded, they were released to a grateful set of families. The nightmare, it seemed, was over.

*

Two weeks after crossing the border, Leigh was back in her dorm room, staring at her laptop. Slowly, she flipped it open and logged in to her Facebook account. There were several frantic posts, mostly asking about her whereabouts. She promptly deactivated the account and set up a new one with no picture. Leigh rose and walked to the closet, cleaning up the various bathing suits and miscellaneous items strewn about.

She placed them in large black garbage bags and threw it in her closet. Almost complete, she sat back at the desk, frowning at the emptiness of her Facebook page. Reloading the page, she noticed a new icon with a start. At the very top of the page, was a friend request. Clicking on it, she saw an unfamiliar name: Jessie Rodriguez. Before she declined it, his profile picture stopped her cold.

Clicking on the thumbnail size, the picture expanded. It was taken in a hotel room. Soft light highlighted the form lying on the bed. She must have been facing the wall, for the picture was taken from behind. Shrouded in linens, her dark hair was tousled, falling in delicate waves on the pillow.

A slow smile crept on her face, and she hit "accept" immediately. While there were only a few pictures of Jessie (in his sunglasses) she noticed suspiciously light blonde hair, and an angle to his chin she found very familiar.

32

"Remind me why we are doing this again?" Eva asked.

Eva and Leigh were primping in a Chicago studio green room, about to go on one of the hottest day time talk shows in existence.

"My hair will not cooperate," glowered Leigh, who had spent an hour, with Eva's assistance, turning her hair into rustic curls.

"You didn't answer my question," Eva responded, smiling, fixing a stray curl on her friend.

"Because, after this appearance we'll have made my father's salary in one day," Leigh said. Eva snickered.

"It's not like we need the money, Leigh."

Leigh met her friend's gaze in the mirror and smiled. They hadn't seen each other as often as they should. It had been two months since spring break and while initially they spoke every day, as summer continued and the heat bore down, they saw each other less and less. But every time they met—every moment they were together—everything was understood.

"What will you do now?" asked Leigh.

"I like it here," Eva said.

"The cold? Eva. Ew."

Eva laughed in response.

"It's just so different than anything I've experienced."

"Did the guy you met at the bar last night have anything to do with that?" Leigh offered. Eva smiled warmly.

"Maybe." They settled into an easy silence. After a few seconds she grabbed Leigh's hand and held it.

"Thank you," she said quietly. Leigh didn't respond. She

looked at her friend and squeezed her hand slightly.

"We did it together," she responded with a smile.

"Ok girls, let's go!" The all too chipper assistant burst in, hustling them out of their chairs and directing them down a long corridor. Leigh blinked as they were brought onto the set, hot lights glaring down on them. They were unceremoniously seated the couch next to the host, who was more beautiful in person than she appeared on the screen.

The lights came on at full blast, and Eva flinched. Leigh leaned next to her and steadied her friend.

"Remember," she whispered, "it was *so very tragic*." After a hustle of lights and cameras, the studio audience twittered to action. They were on camera. The host looked at them both with renewed interest, smiling from ear to ear.

"Today we confront the cartel in our new series, vacation nightmares," began the host, eyelashes batting. "You've read about the courage of these women in the headlines, but what you may not realize is they still are looking for their two friends, the ones who were brutally abducted with them at a popular Cancun resort. Girls, how are you doing after your ordeal?"

The host turned to Eva first, emitting genuine concern. Eva swallowed, then put the full beauty of her long lashes and perfectly styled hair on the crowd.

"It was just, so tragic," she whimpered, as Leigh put a hand on her friend's back. The host nodded, the audience sighed. Flashes of the girls at college parties and sorority functions appeared on the screen. Leigh let Eva do most of the talking, but could not help but smile at the faces of Joy and Gia plastered on the screen.

After the show concluded, the two gathered their free gift bags, and made the trek out of the studio together. After exiting into the parking lot, Leigh turned to Eva.

"You want a ride?"

"I have my bike."

"Such a bad ass," said Leigh.

"You should see me with a gun," Eva shot back. Leigh acknowledged this with a smile.

"Call me. Every once in a while. I know you don't like the phone, but . . . "

"Don't worry, I won't lose touch. Not with you." They shared a brief hug, and Eva departed, easing her bike from its stand.

Leigh watched Eva place her helmet on and expertly zip away, rocketing carefully onto the road. When she was out of sight, Leigh turned towards the dark, tinted car that waited for her.

The chauffeur was kind enough to open the door.

"Thank you," she said, settling in the back of the limo. He entered the driver's side, closing the door and lowering the privacy screen.

"Everything go well, Señorita?"

"Yes. Everything went perfectly."

"Perfecto," Guero replied, taking off his hat, before turning and easing himself through the partition that separated them. Leigh laughed at the sight of him, in his elegant suit and tie, crawling towards her in the back of the car. After a few moments of affection, she interrupted him.

"We can't do this here, people will see."

"That's what the tint is for," he replied, grabbing her waist and pulling her down on top of him. He kissed the soft space behind her ear.

"When are you coming home?" he asked. Leigh closed her eyes.

33

Leigh normally didn't sleep on planes. But her head ached from all the publicity they had been doing and she badly needed some rest. She fell into a dreamless sleep somewhere over Arizona, but awoke when a stewardess leaned across to offer a drink.

She had resigned to herself that restful, innocent sleep, once a weekend ritual, would now be a past indulgence. It was the life she had chosen. After firing off a few texts to Eva, she held her documents firmly in hand. This was the last time she would see the U.S. for a long time, possibly forever. While she was excited for her new life, it was hard leaving Eva.

"I don't think I can ever go back there," Eva said when Leigh broke the news. "But I see why you are."

"You might miss it," Leigh responded, tilting her head with a smile.

"Let's just say I've had my fill of Mexico." Eva looked at Leigh and shook her head.

"In some messed up way, some screwed up plan of the universe, it was all supposed to happen," Leigh had responded.

Deboarding in Cancun, Leigh hastily adjusted her makeup. Despite dropping off to sleep, everything was still expertly applied. As soon as the humidity hit her, the smell of the jungle consumed her, she no longer felt tired. She was on edge, ready for the adventure to begin.

*

Walking off the plane, she approached immigration and handed the handsome agent her passport.

"Business trip, Señorita?" That was the first time anyone had asked her that.

"Yes," she responded. "La Playa resort, ever heard of it?"

"Yes, the best." He looked at the passport and back at her again. Leigh saw a slow smile creep across her face.

"Are you the . . . you aren't the . . ." Leigh tried to look nonchalant. "You aren't the girl who was kidnapped, are you?"

"No," Leigh responded, "I'm not that girl."

He studied her for a moment and handed the passport back.

After collecting her luggage, she walked toward customs on practiced heels, her black dress snaking dangerously upward. She pulled the dress down, emitted a swear word, and smiled at the man waiting for her just across the customs line. She watched as the checkpoint lights flashed in front of her.

Red or green.

Stop or go.

The tourists went in a line before her, pushing the button and walking forward. Finally, it was her turn. Smiling, she pressed the button.

Green.

After crossing the threshold she walked towards Guero with a smile. Leigh placed her bag down before him, which he whisked up with one hand, grabbing her by the waist with the other.

Leigh laughed, she was home.

*

www.ingramcontent.com/pod-product-compliance
Lightning Source LLC
Chambersburg PA
CBHW060809120626
46557CB00001B/149